A STAT]

C000176815

Penelope Gilliatt
Born in 1932, Penelope (_____,
screenplays and film critiques. She is perhaps best known for the
original screenplay of *Sunday, Bloody Sunday* (1971). Her novels
include *One by One* (1965). *A State of Change* came two years later.
She died in 1993.

Ali Smith's first novel, *Free Love*, won the Saltire First Book Award.
She is also the author of *Like* (1997); *Other Stories And Other Stories*
(1999) and *Hotel World* (2001). *The Accidental* (2005) won the 2005
Whitbread Novel of the Year.

A State of Change

A State of Change

Penelope Gilliatt

FOREWORD BY ALI SMITH

CAPUCHIN CLASSICS

CAPUCHIN CLASSICS
LONDON

A State of Change

First published in 1967

This edition published by Capuchin Classics 2009

© Angela Conner 1967
2 4 6 8 0 9 7 5 3 1

Capuchin Classics
128 Kensington Church Street, London W8 4BH
Telephone: +44 (0)20 7221 7166
Fax: +44 (0)20 7792 9288
E-mail: info@capuchin-classics.co.uk
www.capuchin-classics.co.uk

Châtelaine of Capuchin Classics: Emma Howard

ISBN: 978-0-9559602-7-7

Foreword

'One of our really distinctive talents, a true original,' Rebecca West said of Penelope Gilliatt. 'She does not turn away from the dark disorder of existence but defiantly brings to bear on it a powerful intelligence, a benevolent wit, passion, style and pure sanity. She leaves us exhilarated,' William Shawn wrote. 'As a critic and journalist,' Katharine Whitehorn commented after Gilliatt's death in 1993, 'she was one of the most sparkling personalities of her time.' Yet only fifteen years after her death almost all of Penelope Gilliatt's work is out of print and she is hardly remembered by the reading public.

So much for posterity, then: you can sense the sanguine Gilliatt shoulder-shrug at what happens when intelligence, adaptability and versatility meet, head on, the stupefying shortness of cultural memory. As a writer that's what she was: immensely clever, adaptable, versatile and likeably urbane; a writer of novels, short stories, a great deal of wide-ranging critique, even an opera libretto, and an award-winning Oscar-nominated screenplay for John Schlesinger's *Sunday Bloody Sunday* in 1971, probably the piece of work she is most remembered for (and, as she wrote in her introductory essay to the script's publication, 'a straight progression from a novel of mine that had lately came out, *A State of Change*'). In the 1960s she'd also strutted the boards at the *Observer* as twin cultural commentator with Kenneth Tynan, Gilliatt on cinema and Tynan on drama (except, fascinatingly, for when they temporarily took on each other's critical roles). After this she went to the States and was a staff writer on the *New Yorker*, where she and Pauline Kael split the cinematic year between them, an ideal arrangement giving Gilliatt time to write her fiction, which she'd begun pursuing in the mid-sixties.

Alongside her several very poised collections of short fiction, and a critical oeuvre ranging from monographs on French cinema directors Jacques Tati and Jean Renoir, to essays on cinema, theatre, music-hall and the nature of comedy, she produced five distinctive novels, of which *A State of Change* (1967) was her second. Each of these is characterised by her sharpness of ear and eye, her great wit, her discursive fictional structure, and her always pertinent, never prescriptive, commentary about the joins and the cracks between history, contemporary culture, and perceptions of these. *A State of Change* packs a particular Gilliatt-like punch, one whose combination of calmness, subtlety, humaneness and blasting intelligence epitomises the great powers of this writer.

Penelope Gilliatt was born in 1932 in London; her mother, Mary Douglass, and her father, Cyril Conner (who worked his way up from lower-class roots to become a barrister and a BBC Radio controller), both came from Newcastle and had family connections with the north-east shipping trade. They bequeathed her her great understanding of the shifts, connections, prejudices and goals of the British class system; much of her writing, too, plays on the differences and connections between the north and the south in Britain and reveals her own great affection for and knowledge of Northumberland, where she and her younger sister, Angela, spent some of their time growing up (her sister later became a renowned sculptor).

The young Gilliatt was a brilliant pianist and was sent to the Juilliard School in New York. But the strain of performance left her unwell and anorexic; she went to college in Vermont instead, then returned to London when she won a *Vogue* talent contest, part of the prize for which was a journalism job with *Condé Nast*.

Red-haired and vivacious, 'chic, petite, almost pixie-like, with a wicked smile, vivid wit. . . she became a star of the media scene that was just emerging as "swinging London", Katharine Whitehorn remembered. Left wing all her life, she was also one of the founder members of the Anti-H-Bomb Committee Of 100, and marched against nuclear proliferation with her first husband, the neurosurgeon Roger Gilliatt. She left Gilliatt in the 1960s for the playwright John Osborne, with whom she had a daughter; when this marriage ended in 1968, she went to the States with her daughter Nolan. In her later years she became alcoholic and her work suffered greatly; her very first novel, *One by One* (1965), is poignant in this hindsight, a story of an apocalyptic London in the grip of a fatal epidemic, whose symptoms have the appearance of severe alcoholism.

It is reputed that Penelope Gilliatt had a higher IQ than that of Einstein, and it's interesting that in all her copious journalism it's very hard to find anything much actually about Gilliatt herself; she seems a bit wrong-footed when she interviews Buster Keaton and he starts asking her questions back about her. We know, for instance, that she was very slim because in her book on Jean Renoir and his films, Renoir, in interview, notices it, comments on how she'd have found surviving the war easy, being so 'easy to ration,' then breaks off into a perfect war anecdote about how he (the son of the Impressionist painter, Auguste Renoir) hired a car just before the fall of Paris, filled its boot with priceless Cezanne canvases and drove them safely to the Midi. This is just one of the examples of how Gilliatt's use of the self, present and observant yet one step removed, allowed her subject the space to talk – the sense of her subject's voice, her subject's self, in her interviews and monographs, is always whole and intimate. Likewise, a reader of her work will only find out how linguistically skilful she herself was by reading an off-the-cuff remark in an interview Gilliatt did with Nabokov: 'we spoke together in several languages. . . I think he was startled and gleeful to find someone out of the blue who spoke Russian.'

Like all the best critics she pretty much keeps herself out of the picture in her critical work; this generosity gives her the gift of a liberated and unpartisan observation; as she commented on Buster Keaton's work, 'Keaton's characters are outsiders in the sense of spectators, not nihilists or anarchists.' Her cinema and theatre criticism reads like a kind of intellectual florescence. Glenda Jackson is, to Gilliatt, 'the only Ophelia I had ever seen who was capable of playing Hamlet.' She saw, in *Waiting for Godot*, an equally strong benign ambiguity: 'Beckett's characters are anything but pure-dyed pessimists: like most people in real life, they are capable of feeling at one and the same time that existence is both insupportable and indispensible, and that they are both dying and also amazingly well.' She was one of the few critics to notice, on its release, how good Kubrick's *2001* is. Her perceptiveness about Arthur Miller is a relief, 'sometimes so sentimental as to be unintelligent'; she spotted a strong class impetus in Hitchcock's work, the "wonderful vivacity of social report" in his early British films; and she wrote with grace about Chaplin, for whom comedy 'is choreography: placing, movement, the intricate classical disciplining of vulgar energy.'

She was always profoundly interested in 'wits, comics, disturbers of the peace' (the subtitle to her 1973 collection of essays, *Unholy Fools*), revealingly articulate on Cary Grant's 'style of unwounding mockery' and superb on Katherine Hepburn, whose 'faultless technical sense makes one feel that she could play a scene with a speak-your-weight machine and still turn it into an encounter charged with irony and challenge.' Any reading of Gilliatt's fiction will reveal why she was particularly drawn to the comedic: 'comedy never explains,' is how she put it in one of her last critical books, *To Wit* (1990). In fact, one of her fictional modes is what might be called a mode of unexplaining; she uses an episodic style, sudden time shifts which might seem to court obliquity but actually re-structure narrative reality so that life, and randomness, and especially dialogue, make the world, not plot device or fictional closure. She quotes Renoir in her monograph, *Jean Renoir* (1975): 'in the cinema you can do all too much. For example, when the hero of a modern film has a phobia, you are obliged to explain it by flashbacks: I mean, to go back to the time when he was beaten by his father, or whatever thing is supposed to have had such a result. This freedom can be quite enfeebling.' The affinity between them is clear; in her own work Gilliatt understood just such an aesthetic discipline.

She was particularly shrewd, in her critical journalism, about the new British cinema and theatre of the 1960s. She found Richard Lester's *A Hard Day's Night* 'the first film in England that has anything like the urgency and dash of an English popular daily at its best. . . produced under pressure, and the head of steam behind it has generated something expressive and alive.' On Joe Orton's 'slumberous savagery' in *Entertaining Mr Sloane,* 'a revenge tragedy going on among the antimacassars and the doilies,' she is nothing short of brilliant; the troubled language of the text is, she writes, 'like parquet over a volcano: its trouble is the time's, not Orton's in particular. It can't quite find its own voice. Not only the characters but also the text itself seems to be speaking in quotation marks. Nothing is said directly; everything is on the bias, spoken at a tangent to make suspect "sincerity". This may be one of the few specifically modern characteristics. . . the contemporary problem of utterance that belies his work is the problem of his not seeming to mean a word he says.'

A State of Change, very much a critique of words and what they mean, and of Britishness in the 1960s, is concerned straight away with the concepts of seeing and survival. 'Kakia Grabowska, aged twenty-three, cartoonist and citizen of Warsaw, travelled to Moscow in 1949 with an electric lightbulb in case the hotel lamps were too dim for her to draw by, and a bathplug saved from her own house after it was destroyed.' To escape 'the rot of subterfuge,' Kakia comes to England and settles in London, a city 'full of closed circles and bitterness about income tax'. She is a caricaturist because 'any other sort of drawing seemed a suavity, like writing fiction about the corpses not yet buried'. East comes west looking for truth and openness, and what happens? 'Do you think you're any good?' an art editor, only scant pages into the novel, asks this woman who's been through hell and back. 'In Warsaw she had belonged to a class that the Nazis had vowed to wipe off the earth; merely to be bored from nine to five in a menial job was not very much.' Her cartoons, the art editor says, just 'don't add up to a person'.

This is the novel's interest too: what does 'add up to' a person, in history, in art, in life? Gilliatt traces a path through the years from 1949 up to the time of the novel's publication in the late 1960s and examines how this new post-war world looks. It's a very funny novel, even in its gravity and quietness, its own refusal of suavity. Kakia, in her 'style of frosty stoicism,' is one of Gilliatt's comic observers, an outsider, a 'displaced' person. She changes her Polish name to Gibbon, the name of the great 'observer of history'.

The novel also traces the existential shift from a time of war to a time of relative stability. Its concerns are post-war health, rebirth and art – embodied, more or less, in Kakia's two lovers, the fine Gilliatt double-act of Don, the dilletante TV executive, and Harry, the well-meaning obstetrician; she has a passion, in her writing, for three-way relationships, and this is one of her most subtle and benign portrayals of the vicissitudes of such a relationship.

The book's other double-act is a formal one: on the one hand history's darkness and on the other Gilliatt's extraordinary lightness of touch, in a novel whose heroine comes totally alive from the very first elegant sentence, armed only with a single lightbulb, and her own material lightness. *A State of Change* is at one and the same time an excoriating analysis of media cynicism, a profoundly pessimistic view of a dilletante time, a time when 'we should be frightened of ourselves', and a vision of light-footed survival against the odds.

A little like Ivy Compton Burnett in her intellectual drive? A little like Muriel Spark in her economic talent, her way with the ironic sting of a sentence? A little like DH Lawrence in her determination to demonstrate how important the discursive nature is to art and to life? In truth, the Gilliatt combination of verbal elegance, wit, observation, politics, generosity, openness of mind and urbane craft, is unique.

She was a fan of Nabokov's fiction, and quoted, in her own critical work, his comment from *Speak, Memory*: 'in a first-rate work of fiction, the clash is not between the author and the characters, but between the author and the world'. What would Gilliatt have made of the surveillance society we live in now? She would recognise it – she knew it all already; from her first novel onwards she was critiquing spin and soundbite; from the start to the end of her oeuvre she was both mourning the loss of dialogue and celebrating the fact that humans will never ever stop playing with words, testing the borders, giving weight to the seeming insubstantiality of everyday life, and asking the important questions. Redefinition – of words, of love, of history, of societal shape, and of the novel itself – is at the very heart of *A State of Change*.

The subtlety of its open ending, which explains nothing, simply displays the numbness of 1960s culture and the daftness of individual selfishness beside the hard-won revolutions, the crucial communalities of British history of the last hundred years, is – like the novel itself – a piece of structural perfection.

Ali Smith
London, June 2009

Part One

I

Kakia Grabowska, aged twenty-three, cartoonist and citizen of Warsaw, travelled to Moscow in 1949 with an electric light bulb in case the hotel lamps were too dim for her to draw by, and a bath plug saved from her own house after it was destroyed. The bulb was stolen from her suitcases the first day she was in the hotel, presumably at the same time that her drawing portfolios were searched, but two days later it was returned without a word through the *babushka* who sat in the corridor. Kakia was coming back from lunch and found the old woman laying out the bulb ceremoniously in the drawer of the bureau, alongside her drawing paper and the half-eaten core of a pear. The bath-plug was the wrong kind for the bath, which had no means of being closed, as she expected, but that too was taken and she unjustly suspected the *babushka* of the theft, although the old woman would not have done such a thing and behaved to guests protectively. Late at night she would often jerk awake from her doze and bring the girl a glass of tea, clucking at the sight of the drawings and screwing her worn index finger into her temple with concern about the labour of them.

Set to watch a Pole, Kakia's Russian guides expected sarcasm and craft. What she gave them was the company of a buffoon run riot. She overrode their dulled deceits by zest, drinking to history with them, taking off her thin coat to enjoy herself in rooms where garbage was being burnt for warmth, eating too much at meals still poorer than Warsaw's and staying up until five with double-dealing guides whom she even invited into her hotel room while she worked. One morning in a park she bought them a swarm of balloons and they carried them through the streets with shouts of pleasure, patting them between each other and planting kisses on the rubber rumps.

Her drawings, which were printed daily in Warsaw, charmed the more gullible censors and made the puritans disgruntled. It was a time when the centre of the Communist world had passed officially from an object of decorous awe to one of idolatry; to the eye of the orthodox her picture of Moscow was merely as enthusiastic as it should be, but it was expressed with a rapture that bothered the grim like a piece of cinder in the eye. The point was not missed in Poland. She drew the new architecture as though it were beautiful. The silent queues were made to seem full of impudent repartee and the cafés alive with debate. She did an artless series of sketches about conviviality, set in a bar which she gave a sign reading 'Point of Collective Sustenance'; when the Russians looking over her shoulder in the bedroom asked her about this, she said it was meant to show the literary character of bureaucratic Russia compared with the curtness of Polish. The Russians, who were used to being called primitive pigs by the Poles, were glad of the praise and warmed to her. In the scraps of dialogue that went with the drawings she described life in Stalin's Moscow as though it were a holiday in Greece, full of people who felt themselves blessed by history and by an ancient freedom to dissent. But the Poles knew Moscow as a very different sort of society, crippled by its past and ruled by men with the sensibilities of tanks. Her bland, pretty drawings and sunny notes, like messages on the backs of picture postcards, had a meaning clear enough to every Pole with a sense of irony. Her divorced husband, Andrzej, a Catholic Marxist who had married her in a civil ceremony not only because he was a Marxist but also because he thought he was likely to want to erase her from his life, saw very well what she was doing and stored up for it a sophisticated dislike.

Towards the end of her visit she was introduced to a painter, a shy, big man who laughed with wonderful pleasure at something she said, lifting his face like a sea-lion balancing a ball on its nose. The paintings in his exhibition repelled her. They were like recruiting posters or portraits of civic functions. But he must have scented sympathy in her, for he took her away later and showed her some work done in secret. On half a dozen of the paintings in his studio the top layer of canvas could be peeled off, and beneath there were abstractions of roof-tops and chimney stacks and windows. Compared with the others they were inventive and vigorous; and yet there was something just perceptible in them which was also weak and already touched with the rot of subterfuge. She sat raging in his cold studio and he offered her vodka and raised his heavy face at her questions. Later he gave her an old pair of Red Army trousers for warmth and she pulled them in at the waist round her neck like a cheese-bag. She felt a candour and interest coming from him that made her anger at their common situation more lucid. She decided finally then to try to escape it and go perhaps to England, where her mother had once lived for five years. In spite of the practical difficulty of the decision, and, the pain of making it, a good deal of her still felt it to be a glib and tawdry betrayal, and she kept thinking that she had an obligation to tell someone of it, although she knew of no one left alive in Warsaw to care. That night in the hotel with her Soviet witnesses she found it impossible for once to do her stint of drawing in front of them, and instead absurdly kept asking the porters if a letter hadn't come from her husband, though they had scarcely communicated with each other since a bitter quarrel four years before about the Warsaw Uprising. While she was on the old Victorian telephone to the hotel desk, speaking Russian less frigidly than usual and leaning her forehead against the wall, one of the guides thought that perhaps she was homesick and that this was why she seemed elusive. He looked at her thin legs and pointed hipbones and had a moment of wishing that he could feed her up.

II

She arrived in a London that seemed full of closed circles and bitterness about income tax. She had set out for England once before, in 1939, and got no farther than Warsaw railway station. The Germans were moving in and her uncle, who was a dentist, had told his desperate sister that the child must leave at once. The day she was due to go he pulled out her back teeth and replaced them with gold ones so that she would have a little capital with her. He promised to meet her at the railway station that evening to put her on to the train, not trusting her parents to be so practical. Her mother, weeping beyond control told her that she must choose what to take with her. In the heat Kakia was as sensible as possible and packed scarves, socks, her fur coat and galoshes. Later her mother took off her jewellery and stowed it away inside one of her child's gloves. Her father gave her his beautiful gold watch and made a new hole in the strap for her with the point of a pair of dividers from her school geometry set. At the last moment he stuffed her pockets with a set of ivory dominoes that they used to play with together. Then the case suddenly had to be unpacked again to get it to shut and she had to wear the fur coat in the sunshine. Both her parents were crying by then and she told them she would rather go to the station on her own. The elegant, frightened couple as usual did what their child said and she waited alone at the station for two days without food while the last trains pulled out, afraid to move in case her uncle appeared as he had promised and unable to buy a ticket without him because her parents had forgotten to give her any money. When she gave up and tried to go back to them the house had been gutted, and she found none of them again.

'Do you think you're any good?' said the art editor of a magazine in London when she had shown him her portfolio. Her drawings were mostly of Polish faces: melancholy, clever men with women's mouths, an official with a narrow pointed pate and tyres of neck like rolled banknotes, young couples wheeling babies in the park and ageing drifters with pillaged faces who had been imprisoned after the war by the new regime as pro-Fascist for their part against the Nazis in the 1944 Uprising. The editor looked at the drawings without recognition, but something in the line had struck him all the same.

'They're very local, of course. Do you think you're any good yourself?'

'Not yet,' she said precisely. Her English was her mother's, fluent and careful. The man looked as if saying such a thing was an irredeemable mistake. She had heard him being quite as deprecating about himself; it was the basis of his manner. Later on, when he had packed up her drawings and stood her a drink in a Fleet Street pub, she heard the same coinage of self-disparagement over and over again. It took her months to realise that, though it was important in England in 1949 to belittle your achievement, it was ruinous to mean it. Her small claims for herself made her unemployable. The local style of an underlying arrogance was a question of spreading confidence; much power was held by the bankrupt, and they needed credit.

'Why don't you like the drawings?' she said with difficulty later. The man was embarrassed, and laughed to divert the question into banter.

'Why?' she said again,

'They're a bit anatomical, aren't they? I suppose that's it. He had fixed on the very thing that had struck him earlier as possibly good, but she had tipped the situation the wrong way in his office and now he had lost his flash of nerve so that he had to ascribe his instinct to something else. 'And they haven't got enough style.'

'What does that mean? Is it different in England?'

'Not enough lightness. Style means a sort of tact. These seem to – go on a bit. It's hard to put. Do you know what that means? It's an idiom. To go on a bit,'

'No. To go ahead?'

'On no. It means to pile it on. Get hot under the collar. Exaggerate. I know it's probably different in Poland. I mean, it's an exaggerated situation there altogether, isn't it? The whole thing. I don't mean to sound unsympathetic. It's all in the tone of voice in England, you know. I don't mean that literally; I mean the tone of the way one behaves. One puts over one's point of view a lot better here if one doesn't get steamed up about it. Those drawings are a bit unnerving, aren't they? For England! Don't you feel that? But you'll soon get it. You speak English jolly well! Amazing.'

'I don't understand, quite, I'm sorry, what you mean by anatomical.'

'Well –. You make rather too much out of what people look like, don't you? You make them look pretty strong stuff. And at the same time they're too complicated so that you don't quite bring off the thing of making one laugh at them. They are meant to be funny, after all,'

'Not entirely.'

He didn't listen to this. 'You see what I mean. Look at this one. You get an effect one way with this brilliantly funny chin, for instance, which is a splendid baroque ornament, isn't it, and then you cancel it out with this rather involved and fundamentally serious nose. I mean the nose is really quite affable, isn't it? And intelligent. Whereas the chin is pretty asinine. Er, stupid. You did mean it to be stupid, didn't you? The two contradict each other. They don't add up to a person.'

'No?' She was lost. She understood nothing. He might as well be speaking gibberish.

'Well, not in a *cartoon*. I'm not talling about real life. Or art in a garret for that matter. You can go away and be a genius on the assumption I'm wrong but I don't suppose you'd be tramping the streets looking for work if you wanted to blush unseen, would you? Let me put it another way. If you don't simplify, people don't get it. No, simplify's a poor word to use because it implies concessions. What I mean is that all the great caricaturists get the *answers* for people. Ambiguities just don't add up, not in drawings, do they? People want you to do the digging for them. Come up with something. That's the whole secret of cartoons.' She nodded because he looked so pleased and revived by his flailing truisms. 'People want you to look at – Winston, say – and put down a bulldog. British phlegm. How we survived. All that.'

She drew Churchill quickly on the back of a piece of silver cigarette paper. 'He has this mouth, you see,' she said as she did it. 'People never show it because of the cigar. It's very thin. Not because he is thin but because there is weight from his cheeks and pressure from his jaws. The mouth is full of will, and sentimental. He has a colossal forehead. A wardrobe. When he sits, he sits symmetrically with his arms a little back. As if he was on the lavatory. A lot of Russians hold their arms close to their bodies like this. It is because they were swaddled when they were babies. They are wrapped up in bandages all the time.'

'I don't suppose they went in for swaddling much at Blenheim,' he said. She smiled obligingly, having no idea what Blenheim was but guessing it to be funny. He wondered whether to go on, and tried again. 'Look. I wish I could help. If you slave away I'm sure it'll come. Try to lay off the physical element, that's the main thing. We're all pretty hideous, after all. But don't rub it in. It puts people off. We've had enough in England. Not that you haven't in Poland too, of course. You're good at likenesses, aren't you? Poor old Winnie. Perhaps you could do political stuff.'

'These are political, aren't they? The Warsaw drawings.'

'Oh no. These are social.'

'In Poland they're very political.'

'These are a sort of notebook. Jottings. They might be anybody. The great thing for a cartoonist is a nose for the people who make things tick. These don't, do they? These people. They're like – oh, drawings of any old crowd in Woolworth's.'

I don't suppose you know what Woolworth's is.'

'Yes I do. In the Strand. I go and buy notebooks there. I like it. People buying packets of flower seeds.'

Before she went he made her do a drawing of herself, meaning idly to get her to show that she could produce a pleasantry when she didn't try, instead of these knotty complexes of features that never quite allowed him to laugh. He thought she was rather a pretty girl. She caught this in the drawing, but other things as well. She showed that her hair was coarse and shot stiffly out of her scalp like a sink brush. Her mouth was big and uneven and her eyebrows were not arched but angular. Her features looked more obdurate when they were isolated from her light voice. The sketch made him see that her hands were huge, practically the size of her skull, and that she had a very long upper lip that she raised over her front teeth to smile.

'I wish you hadn't done that,' he said involuntarily. 'You've made yourself look like a monkey.

'But I do,' she said.

And then she went on: 'What are the words in English for monkey?'

'What do you mean? I don't know. Ape. Baboon, Gorilla. Why?'

'I can't go on trying to make people understand Grabowska.'

'It's not particularly difficult. You can't call yourself Miss Gorilla.'

'Anyway Grabowska's a name I can't use. It's my husband's. Ex-husband's.'

'Oh, a feminist. I can't think of any other words for you, Gibbon. Why can't you use your maiden name?'

'Zanuszkiewicz?'

She lived in digs off the Strand, partly because she had heard the name in an old English music-hall song that her mother sometimes sang, which made the words 'Strand Palace Hotel' on the cap of a hotel courier at the airport seem venerable and full of welcome, and partly because she could walk to Fleet Street from where she was staying and save the bus fares. It had never occurred to her that she might not be able to do the same sort of work as in Poland. Editors implied that she fitted in nowhere and they were right. The newspapers had their own cartoonists. The literary magazines weren't interested in expressing a point of view through drawings. *Punch* was more hostile to her portfolio than anyone and said that the *Punch* style was comedy of situation, not studies of people. The expensive women's magazines saw a distinction in her work but said apologetically that it didn't tally with anything they needed, which was something with a little more charm to illustrate travel articles or features on entertaining. When she took her work into art departments she sometimes saw the sort of drawings that must have been wanted. They were generally wistful, unassuming, quirky in a gentle and winsome way: shafts of private eccentricity that left no wound, about non-human creatures with muffin faces or noses like beaks or feet the size of snowshoes, put into situations that made people laugh tenderly with their heads on one side as if at babies. There were also the accomplished drawings of landscapes and buildings and gardens; but she wanted to draw faces, and the elegant self-effacement of the high-class English illustrator was something she could never have reproduced even if she had trusted it. 'Light' was the word that editors kept using to her. She grew to hate it, and in the evenings when she worked she drew more and more assertively with a thick-nibbed felt pen, hell-bent on coarsening her piercing and sceptical style into something close to what her languid detractors called it.

Most of the Englishmen she met overcompensated fitfully for what a Pole must have suffered, by being sorry for her for living alone on very little money, but it was a sympathy she did not need. She was used to living nowhere, snatching sleep as if she were looting it and choosing food on the basis of how long it would last her. In a chemist's shop in the Strand she discovered diabetic chocolate, and a liver extract that she ate with a teaspoon in her digs at night instead of a meal. She found an Italian cafe where she could buy a very large piece of home-made apple pie for ninepence, which she ate at noon in the sun in the Embankment Gardens while the band played. Sometimes at lunchtime she went to St Martin's-in-the-Fields, where there were free concerts. She liked walking through the market in Covent Garden. The atmosphere was friendly and caustic and the smells were good. There were always old apples to be picked up and if she went at the right time there was no need to pilfer because one or two of the men were touched by her and freely gave her their leavings anyway.

When it rained she would generally take her apple pie into Lyons. No one seemed to mind her eating it there as long as she bought a cup of tea. Lyons own pies were cheaper but smaller and not as good. The best thing there was the bread; sometimes she bought a penny roll and a twopenny pat of the unfamiliarly salty butter. She could have had two pats of bright yellow margarine for the same price, but it stank of glue or whale and made her feel ill.

After a few weeks, when her money had run out and she had earned nothing, she took a job that she saw advertised in the window of an ancient group of women's magazines. She worked in the home-dressmaking department and fetched the coffee, and felt herself fortunate to earn forty-five shillings a week for it. In Warsaw she had belonged to a class that the Nazis had vowed to wipe off the earth; merely to be bored from nine to five in a menial job was not very much.

Sometimes the people in this run-down, subaqueous office seemed so sealed off in their Englishness, so unaware of it, that she felt herself to be almost spying on them. Her place was at a desk half-hidden behind a filing cabinet in a tiny room that was used as a corridor into the office beyond. Her boss, who edited crochet leaflets and a sewing magazine, was a tall, intimidated woman with narrow crouching shoulders and big hips who lived at Tottenham. Her name was Miss Fox, and when the house telephone buzzed she would pick it up and say simply 'Fox' as if she were a man. Years ago – twenty, thirty years ago – she had modelled her voice and her clothes on the editor-in-chief's, a woman called Miss Sylvia Boddenham whose phone calls Kakia could recognise through the perpetually open door because Miss Fox's voice grew frightened and shrill. After the calls Miss Boddenham would generally speed into the office herself to push the thorn farther in. She was a frailly made woman who had her couture tweed suits finished with taffeta linings that cracked like sails in a wind when she was in a bullying mood. Her deep pink fingernails were very long and they curled over at the edges. She wore toques and cartwheel hats in the office, on top of fine creamy peroxided hair that was piled up under the hats. Cream was her favourite colour. She called it 'top-o'-the-milk' and her office was painted in it every year, with air conditioning installed to save the dirt of open windows. Elsewhere the offices were filthy and the light fitments on the staircase had had the bulbs removed to save electricity bills.

'I'm tyrannical about accessories,' she said once with a mistaken collusiveness to Kakia, trying to win her love by allowing her to take a lace handkerchief out of her bag. Kakia had no idea of the currying purpose of this manoeuvre and noticed only that the bag inside was too tidy and empty of personality. The fact that it was made of crocodile was a local signal of lofty taste that meant nothing to her. Miss Boddenham's bags and shoes were always of crocodile, and when she pushed through the office she generally had in her hand the quill pen that she used for writing copy. Miss Fox also wore hats in the office, but hers were made of poor felt or yellowing chip straw, and her imitations of Miss Boddenham's suits were tight and turned shiny by the office chair. Her hair, which she tried to do like the editor's, grew wispily down her neck and kept falling out from under her hat. When she was abused by Miss Boddenham the blood would rise in her cheeks and her hesitant speech would sometimes run into a pitiful lock. After the editor had gone away, smelling of lilies of the valley and smiling avidly at Kakia behind the filing cabinet, Miss Fox would sit still for a few minutes and then come out to Kakia and ask her to go into the Strand for some groceries or food for her dog. Or she would telephone to the art department, whom she called 'the boys', and the middle-aged art editor would come down to talk to her and have a cup of tea and a Chelsea bun that Kakia fetched for them from the cafe next door.

Kakia was always repaid for what she got if it was for Miss Fox, but when she had to fetch elevenses for a conference in Miss Boddenham's room she was often five or six shillings out of pocket. Miss Fox had a silver teaspoon of her own that she kept in her pencil tray, because she didn't like the cafe's plastic spoons, and even when she was distressed she ate her Chelsea bun neatly, unfurling the bread and putting the coil onto a piece of typewriting paper and blotting her panicky red lips on a hemmed handkerchief. Sometimes Kakia heard her crying as she talked. The art editor, who was kind to her, had been there even longer than she had and was given less pain by the place; Miss Boddenham's evil tactics had the effect on him of making him sarcastic and lazy, and his rows with her were conducted with a dapper chill. Though he despised the contents of the magazines, which were mostly instructions for fussy home-made clothes and paragraphs about entertaining written for the printers by Miss Boddenham in copperplate, it seemed to Kakia that he had a good deal of acid relish in handling the poor material that she brought up to him.

'Ah, a hug-me-tight,' he said one day, using a pair of pincers to pick out the letters of the word and laying it out in an ecclesiastical typeface. 'The hug-me-tight is going to be the spirit of the turn of the decade. The nineties had Aubrey Beardsley. We have the hug-me-tight.' He knew that his exhausted, aghast voice took her off the hook. 'I don't suppose you ever heard of the hug-me-tight in Poland, did you? First the cardigan became the bolero, and then the bolero progressed into the hug-me-tight. A far cry from the austerity of the jumper. In the war it was all jumpers. Not sweaters. Sweaters are American. We aren't allowed to have anything Yankee in this office. Miss Boddenham doesn't like it. Do you know the definition of utility underclothes? One Yank and they're off. Utility was the name for wartime ugly, the goods they pumped out in a peculiarly hideous style of patriotism, though better than what you had I daresay. Definition of a utility table: thick legs and no drawers. No, you don't understand that. Drawers are undergarments. Of an old-school sort, and rather underprivileged now I suppose. You could say that Miss Fox wears drawers, perhaps. Not Miss Boddenham. Miss Boddenham would wear something daintier. Hand embroidered, no doubt, by nuns in Belgium, or perhaps by her secretary.'

The way he talked gave very little indication of his goodwill. He protected himself and won a reputation by seeming satanic, but Kakia received his support and affection, and she once caught him giving tea in Lyons to Miss Boddenham's secretary on a bad day when the manicurist had broken one of Miss Boddenham's nails and the circulation of the magazines had once more dropped.

This haunted man – his name was Ambrose Foster – whose sense of himself had become stagnant and brackish, had long ago stopped supplying any such affection to his own life. As a young man he had been talented, but now he was unaccountably a disappointment. Why? He thought himself that it was sloth. Others attributed it to his secretiveness, his homosexuality, his rasping tongue, his maiden sister. The visible aspects of his life were sackcloth and his method of dealing with them was to find them droll. But though he thought of himself as a spectator, the things he mocked had almost consumed him; he joked lazily about the absurdities of the magazines, but the truth was that they constituted his only mythology. When he spoke of the issues that the firm had turned out in the war he became as possessive as anyone in the office. The war, their war, was even still bodily present in the scraps of blackout material left under drawing pins at the tops of the window frames, and in the paths of glue left by the safety tape against flying glass that had been put across the panes in 1939. Ambrose had been found unfit for call-up, and he had worked here through the blitz like every other underpaid senior milk-pony still in the building. The staff talked endlessly and nostalgically of features about balaclava helmets for the forces, and about carrying blocks of illustrations from the engravers to the printers through the bombs.

The reminiscences implied that the magazines were somehow different then: more urgent, more significant. Yet when Kakia had to go down to the vaults to look up the dusty old bound volumes for some reason or other, the wartime issues were exactly the same as the present ones. They had the same Boddenham paragraphs, the same nagged and cautious clothes, the same ogling captions. World slaughter had induced in them no more reality or charity than the present doldrum times. There was the same legend of a life of entertaining and smart functions and supper parties on satin-stitched tablemats, endlessly reproduced by faithful, timid people who lived alone in Tottenham with a dog. Ambrose mocked it, discarded it, but savoured it all the same as if it made a satisfactory metaphor for his own absurdity. He had adopted a nihilsim with a course of pain in it somewhere which he forebade one to try to locate. The two single things that he took seriously, and did not speak about, were talent in painting and the spectacle of effort in others. Occasionally he asked to see the work that Kakia was doing. He edged her away from the surplus vehemence that had come into it because of criticism, and she started to draw more freely without realising his impetus. London engrossed her. She dwelt endlessly on something that she found in English faces, a last-ditch energy and hunger for risk that was quite different to the imperturbable conventionality of the truisms. There was hardly a face she saw that did not seem to her to be gigantically thrown out of true, the result of eruptions and landslides, with an enormous nose or a jutting chin or a grotesquely underhanging lip. English faces to her were like illustrations of the medieval humours, and the efforts of the owners to standardise them by putting them under matching bowler hats or county felts or dull straws skewered with hat-pins only made them less uniform and more startling. She drew Ambrose's face again and again. He had a thin mouth, a big high nose with skin stretched tightly over the bridge, an upper lip and chin that formed a straight slope in profile, and the gasping nostrils of a landed fish.

She went to Liverpool Street Station and drew farm workers in teddy-boy clothes up for the evening by train from Essex. They looked scrubbed and strong, and more keenly differentiated than any nationality she had seen: one of them with a profile like the conventional idea of an ambassador, one like a Leonardo warrior with a howling mouth, one a costive dog with cheeks like panniers and eyes that sloped down at the outer edges. Her drawings were fierce because they were made in the context of what she knew, which was Warsaw slowly razed to the ground, a city where she had eventually lived in rubble and survived by inventing a mendacious life in an office that gave her a work-card and the opportunity to operate on the black market. She had started to do caricatures because any other sort of drawing seemed a suavity, like writing fiction about the corpses not yet buried. She developed unconsciously an ethic of pressure and crudity, and in exile she went on obeying it, charging the woebegone class differences and stuffy public attitudes and unjoined wars of post-war England with the ferocity that they invisibly possessed. The public-school stockbrokers whom she drew in City restaurants appeared to her to be not fatuous but fighting for their lives, and she assumed that they were prepared to do it ugly. When she went to the provinces at the weekends she found people who apparently belonged to other countries. She drew poor women whose humour and capability seemed to her beyond epithets. She watched roaring old men at football matches and young men with big knees like dray horses, wearing navy blue double-breasted pin-stripe suits for Sunday that they sat in as if they were egg shells. She did many drawings of old people, without pathos, obsessed by the hermits' stratagems in their faces. Her humour was grim, but it was not about grievance. It was a style of frosty stoicism, absorbed with death not as a romantic theme but as the cliff face on which it had to find a purchase.

III

That Christmas Ambrose asked her to his flat for the day. He had the top floor of a house in Battersea that overlooked the river, and his sister the floor below. It was a curious day: half celebratory, half bashful, with the English people suddenly made aware of their habits by the presence of a foreigner and blustering a little about what they called their nonsensical Christmas customs as if they had no responsibility for them. Ambrose and his sister, who were high Anglicans, reserved their feelings about Christmas to themselves. Apart from these two there was no one in the room who was religious, nor had anyone any children who might have supplied the usual acceptable reason for atheists to make something of Christmas. Yet there was a tree with lights on it standing on the raised slate hearth, and a row of beautiful stars and gold cobwebs and Japanese paper fish twisting on nylon thread from a girder in the ceiling; and Ambrose's sister had cooked a goose as well as a turkey. The fact that she herself was a vegetarian was somehow typical of the day.

Some people there felt constrained by the feast, as if they were involved in an absurdity. Others were impatient to have had a useless holiday thrust on them that was tamer than ten English Sundays put together. Others were wretchedly aware of the tradition of asking lame dogs to Christmas dinner, each suspecting the dog to be himself. Yet all the same, in practically everyone at the party there was some feeling of jubilance as well, as though the day were liable to be a good one if only because trouble was being taken.

The first thing that Kakia saw when she came in was the light from a window that looked on to the river, with the silhouettes of two young men against it. They were bent towards each other and talking, leaning in identical positions against the return walls of the window-recess, with their hips braced against the walls and their legs crossed in front of them and their hands in their pockets. The tops of their bodies were angled away from the walls so that their heads were close together. Against the light she could hardly see their faces; it was their shapes that were distinctive, and later this was the way she always remembered them, like the two halves of a walnut shell in the act of splitting.

'Thank heavens you haven't brought me anything, dear,' said Ambrose when he had let her in. 'Apart from your zoo. Do you always travel with your zoo?' But it was a present for him: two white birds in a cage that she had bought in Camden Town, and he was very pleased. She had done a drawing of the birds on a white sack of seed and this pleased him too. 'Now I shall have to put a piece of tinsel round a packet of Players for you,' he said. But in a corner of the room there was a hammock, obviously used generally for reading and looking out at the river, and today it was full of cardboard boxes wrapped in tinfoil containing huge paper flowers that he had made.

When the flowers were given to people no one quite knew what to do with them. His mother an abstracted woman sitting by the fire who made disjointed pronouncements as though she were on a badly connected trunk call, used the stalk of hers at times to run beneath her hair and scratch her head. A girl in jeans lying in a wicker cocoon chair, almost hidden under a white fur rug that she had taken off the floor, was twirling her flower against the light. She scarcely opened her mouth all day and Kakia couldn't make up her mind whether she was sullen, thoughtful, or perhaps even mightily drunk. After she had watched her for a while she thought it was probably a performance of teenage daze and that the girl was twenty-seven at least. The reason why her face was unlined was perhaps that no expression ever passed through it, the owner having developed a reputation for herself as a sort of delphic presence simply by a habit of non-participation that had begun as a defence against the efforts of a boisterous English nanny to boot her into vivacity. As a child she had eluded the punishment of being sent to bed without supper by going to sleep, and the device was so successful that in later life she elaborated it. Her silences were neither benevolent or malign; they were quite neutral, a position, a crow's nest in the upper air where she had posted herself long ago in the pretence of being a look-out and slowly, slowly slipped off her perch with boredom. When she happened to be sitting between two people who were communicating with each other her presence had a peculiar effect, like a freezing current of air that was suddenly chilling their legs, blown from a place where there was too little oxygen to think.

Just before lunch she suddenly got up and walked away to Ambrose's bedroom and slept. People could see her curled up under an eiderdown, but no one did anything about it. Kakia has never met anyone like her. Such cultivated anonymity in an English girl who was, so people told her, well-known and popular, puzzled her completely. What rewards of company did she offer? Kakia was used to spongers, but the ones she knew were more active. How did this girl live? Was she alone? Unhappy? As far as she emanated anything she emanated a suggestion of not being married, or at any rate of being equally non-attached to everyone in the room. Yet in the middle of lunch she came back with a baby under her arm like a kitbag and looked as if she were preparing to feed it at the table, drawing up a chair beside a doctor who had green eyes and a low, warm way of speaking. The doctor stopped talking at once and frowned and clenched his shoulders as though he were willing his wife not to open her shirt. Ambrose's sister, Eliza, looked distressed at the foot of the table but kept silent.

'Not with the goose,' said Ambrose, moving a lighted candle away from the baby, whose downy scalp was within a few inches of it. The baby started to cry and its father carried it about spreadeagled face downwards on his forearm. It was so small that it scarcely reached from the crook of his elbow to his palm. The baby stopped crying, stared at the floor for a time and went to sleep. 'She's not hungry, darling,' he said to his wife, and took the baby away again to the bedroom. On his way back he picked up his wife's cat, which was pawing the bird cage, and shut it in the bathroom.

This was one of the two men whom Kakia had seen standing in the window. His name was Harry Clopton. His friend sitting opposite him and watching the baby with an impatient expression, was a man in television called Don Clancy. At first they looked rather alike, but it was only their height and their Italian tweed jackets and the way their hair was cut. They had known each other slightly in the army and then been at Oxford at the same time as a medical student and an English student they ought not have met, but Don's instinct to lead several separate lives at once had made him sometimes quit his cronies in the debating union to try out another sort of existence with the serious young man who ate on his own in tea rooms instead of boisterously in hall. Don's contemporaries, who tended to be bewitched by rum, were as intrigued and misled by his disappearances as they were by his presence. There was something immediately extravagant and legendary about rum, even as an undergraduate.

He was the only person Harry had ever met who seemed to have absolutely no past. Most people Harry knew were more or less formed and punished by their history; Don alone seemed free of it and to have been born without kin or remorse, and

Harry admired this as if it were some sublime facility, like
finding it easy to entertain people or to argue well. Don argued
as compulsively as he used the telephone and even his quarrels
seemed blithe. Far from forcing themselves into his mood later
and leaving him spent, they seemed to give him a sense of dash.
He dealt with ideas entirely aphoristically, in a way that
made them symmetrical and replete, instead of open to the
interference of a doubt. At Oxford he had loved making absurd
sexual epigrams about politics, like 'Democracy would work if
one could imagine the Statue of Liberty in bed.' He had a way of
talking in goading formulations instead of asking questions,
and he would never have allowed himself the sort of burbles
that Harry drifted into when he was happy or looking for
something he had mislaid. Generally Harry was rather taciturn,
but when he was trying to find something – half of a pair of
shoes, or a textbook – a fit of loquacity would often come onto
him and if there was anyone in hearing he would talk fitfully
and rather inaudibly as he bent in and out of cupboards. Don
struck him as remarkable partly because he was someone who
genuinely had a gift for being modern instead of feeling a little
at odds with his time. What Don couldn't do, he saved himself
by not wanting to do. He couldn't drive a car, for instance, or
hold drink, and after Harry had known him a while he realised
that he didn't find it easy to get on with girls; but he managed
enviably to invent substitutes for his lacks, whistling up taxis
with an air, drinking very little apart from carefully chosen
wines and cultivating an indifference to girls that left them
trotted and full of longing. He himself was most stirred by
indifference and brazenness. Apart from Harry, he always
associated quality with audacity and insolence; the probity that
he sensed in Harry was the most substantial thing in his own
life and he knew it, but it was out of key with the other objects
of his admiration. It therefore became the one thing that he
refrained from analysing, because he knew instinctively that the

self-addressed simplicity of Harry's temperament would have called too many other aspects of his own life into question. Otherwise his ideal companion was a very English type of nerveless and highly-educated mocker, insubordinate, plausible, specious and irresistibly destined to fall on his feet. The fact that the confidence Don worshipped in others was something he often destroyed in them gave his life something secretly barren and poignant, and it was this that Harry responded to in him much more than to his sparkling intelligence, which was finally not very deep running or speculative. He was a man who seemed rather alarmingly an artefact, a self he had chosen to be; his talents and his gait and his way of speaking seemed to have been invented by him, not to have evolved organically. This flair of the will, and his talent for power, struck his contemporaries as a sort of genius. But in the end, as he well knew himself, it did not amount to the creative imagination that he longed for, but to a gift for deduction and brilliant imitation. Whenever he was being most dazzling to people he always had in his mind that he was only improving on some trait or notion that he had admired in someone else, and this would distress him so much that the thought of it had to be hidden. It was at moments like this that Harry meant most to him. Harry gave others a sense of solace and aplomb simply because he was a first-hand man.

Even the sight of him raised one's spirits. Though he was a doctor he dressed unconventionally. He liked brightly coloured ties and Italian jackets, and to signal his contempt for depression he kept growing moustaches and beards and sideburns of different sorts, tending them lovingly and always slicing them off before anyone had got used to them. Don would have liked to have copied them. At present Harry had a beard, and Don unconsciously kept fingering his own chin. Kakia could see that Harry's wife struck Don as embarrassing. She was a blunder in the pantheon. His own hunger for the best obtainable was so restive and relentless that acquiescence by a hero in anything less rocked his confidence. It was like an acrobat's foot slipping; it genuinely frightened him.

'You've not had any turkey,' he said to Harry's wife accusingly when the baby had been settled to sleep again. She shook her head and smoked her cigarette.

'The King managed his stammer very well,' said Ambrose's mother suddenly. She had made everyone stand up earlier for the Royal speech to the Empire on the radio. Don instantly told a story about a learned Scottish professor with a stammer who had once been stopped dead in the middle of a word in front of a group of acolytes while he was watching a firework display at the Edingburgh Festival. '"W-w-w," stuttered the professor,' said Don, leaning forward and mimicking the effort with a literalness that Harry found painful. 'The students looked away and tried to do something else. "W-w-w," he said. "Wordsworth?" said someone. "W-w-w-w," he said angrily. "Wilkes?" said someone. The professor shook his head. Another rocket went up and they all fixed their eyes on it and wondered what piece of scholarship was trying to get out. "W-w-whoosh," he said.'

'What?' said Ambrose's mother.

'It's a story about a clever man who was only trying to say "whoosh", mother,' said Ambrose's sister deliberately. The reason why she spoke slowly was that she had had a stammer herself as a child and had learned to control it by taking her time. She caught her mother's eye and hoped desperately that she wouldn't mention it.

'It's not a very funny story,' said Mrs Foster, with some mercy. 'I don't suppose our guest understood it.' Harry said that he would like some more turkey and smiled at Kakia as he passed his plate, saying 'If Don suggests playing any of his awful academic parlour games I'll go mad.' They were the next thing he could see coming. Instead Don started making formulations about Communism, which Ambrose eventually stopped by saying that he couldn't understand them. A skeletal model girl with a colossal appetite turned out to be unexpectedly lewd and told a row of very good limericks. Don declined the mood and came back to his own themes.

'I mistrust a country like Russia where the obscenity is all in the invective and none in the humour.'

'Oh, is that true?' said Kakia. 'I suppose it is. But then Poles aren't very fair to Russians.'

'I thought you were all Slavs,' said an elderly photographer comfortably.

'Not quite,' said Kakia.

Don tried to get her to talk about the difference by defining it himself, but she was alert to his mechanism by now and merely grinned at him blandly. Harry caught the grin for a moment and looked very clearly pleased with her. After they had all had some Stilton and built up the fire they played demon patience on the floor; Harry's wife turned out to be unexpectedly good and won again and again. Then the baby started crying and she disappeared into the bedroom to feed it, and the rest of them lay in the hammock and on the fur rugs and drank soda water and China tea. Kakia talked most of the time to Ambrose's sister, who wanted to go to an art exhibition with her. She seemed genuinely interested. There was something about the care of her speech that was absorbing and attractively dispassionate. The sun went down and the fire shone on the decorations and the river outside looked like mercury, thick and sliding.

It suddenly reminded Kakia that she had brought with her a little ball of lead that she had carried around in her pocket since the beginning of the war. It had been given to her by a Latvian maid who used to boil it up at Christmas in a little saucepan and then drop it into cold water to make shapes and tell fortunes. Kakia had thought she might do it for people herself, hoping it would amuse them, but Harry steered her off, not because he thought it was superstitious of her but because he knew that it would incite Don's derision.

'Do it for the baby,' he said easily. 'Look, Sal, it's made a bowler hat. Your little girl's going to be a stockbroker.' Wasn't the child his, then? Kakia had seldom seen a man look so fond of a baby, and she put the phrase down to another of the many English idioms that implied disavowal. But as it happened she was right. Sal Clopton had had a sleepy and pain-dealing affair with a conman who had rooked her and gone to gaol, and the child was his.

'Can I give you a lift?' said Don, edging her into a corner. 'Wouldn't you like to have supper?' She was surprised; she had had a strong impression that he disliked her. Why was he whispering? 'What about the others?' she said.

'I've got to go into Alexandra Palace for a few minutes. You could come in and see the studios. Then we could have a Chinese supper and forget Christmas.' He raised his eyebrows. She was being edged into a conspiracy of mocking the day that she didn't actually support; she had enjoyed herself. But she couldn't think of any excuse strong enough to stand up to his persuasion, so she agreed. It was the first of many occasions when she was parked somewhere by Don for what he called 'a few minutes' and left like a dog on trust for a very long time. Alexandra Palace that evening was like a luxury liner that had been cleared because of a bomb-scare. By the time they left Don said that he didn't really know where to go for dinner at Christmas and perhaps she could cook him something at home if she was hungry?

Before they had left the flat, Kakia had seen that Harry had observed everything in spite of Don's ploys. She heard him explaining to Ambrose's mother, who had sharp ears and an incredulous nature, that Chinese restaurants really were sometimes open on Christmas Day.

'Why don't you go with them?' the old woman had said loudly to Harry.

'I think Sal's tired,' he had replied, looking as if he rather wanted to.

'Can I telephone for a taxi?' Don had said. The photographer had said that he was taking the model girl home to stoke her up with a bit more starch, and the model girl had said affably that she could find her own way, thank you very much.

'To find one's own way is Titoism,' Ambrose's mother had said decidedly to the fire.

IV

Four and a half years later, in the early summer of 1954, Harry Clopton took the night sleeper from Paris to Rome to read a paper at a medical conference. In the corridor of a second-class carriage when he was trying to find the restaurant he found his way blocked by Kakia. She had her eyes shut and looked as if she were waiting for a noise to be over. After a few moments he realised from her breathing that she was asleep. He sat down on her suitcase, which was in the corridor beside her, and watched her for a time until she woke. She recognised him at once.

'I'm so sorry. I was in the way.'

'You sleep like a horse, don't you? Standing up.'

'How do you remember me?'

'I suppose you must be in my mind because Don asks me about you. He seems to think we meet all the time for some reason.'

'Does he really do that? He keeps asking me if I've seen you. Why?'

'Because we've had a long history of my swiping his girls. I never mean to. The difficulty is that he's so secretive that I never know they *are* his girls until too late. Before I got married he used to take Sal out. I only discovered a long time afterwards. Where are you going to?'

'He saw me off, and he made me promise to telephone from Paris. He said he'd be sure to be in, but when I got through no one knew where he was. Will he think I haven't done it?'

'He might pretend to if he thought he could make something of it. But I shouldn't think he can do that to you, can he? Blackmail you like that?'

'Sometimes.'

'One has to remember that he goes as far as people let him. That's how he finds out what they're like. He does it instead of asking questions, I think. He tries people out. To find out how they're made. Other people really are mysterious to him, you know. I think he feels as if everyone else has some secret. Does it bother you? I daresay it must.'

'I like him very much.' She paused. 'But I always feel I'm disappointing him. As if I'm not as good as the time before.' She paused again, and then opened her packet of Gauloises and offered him one.

'Should we have dinner? Would it be a good idea?' This was one of the phrases that Harry Clopton used: a good idea; he thought about small decisions carefully, as if they were projects that might be important. 'Or do you want to be on your own?'

'Dinner on the train. I'd love to. Love to.' She smiled hugely and her long upper lip rose over her teeth. He thought it looked pretty. 'Wait a minute while I do my hair.' She opened her bag and he saw there was a banana in it and a tube of toothpaste. 'Meals on trains. Everyone likes eating on trains. Meals on aeroplanes taste as if your tongue is hanging out of the window.'

'It's the air hostesses I don't like.'

'I thought men were supposed to love air hostesses. I thought that was what they were for.'

'They've got the bad side of nurses without being sweet and kind and sexy. They're like nurses because they're bossy, and vaguely frightening at the same time as being niminy-piminy. But unlike nurses, not sexy. Why? They can turn an aeroplane into a sort of airborne doily department, and all the time you think you may be going to die.'

'I didn't know a doctor ever saw nurses that way.'

'The wing could be falling off, and all an air hostess would do when you asked about it would be to smile and tidy up your paper cup. The way they say "We hope you have enjoyed flying with us, and look forward to seeing you again." As if they'd ever *recognise* you again. I always expect to hear that voice in hospital on the tannoy. "Your pilot and Miss Belvedere and I hope you have enjoyed your operation, and thank you for flying with us." Do you think there's a smile school for air hostesses? If they could really fly the thing. Or if they'd actually cooked the stuff, or even if they were allowed to go out with the passengers. They're entirely anti-functional, aren't they? And I'm afraid they know it. I expect that's why they're so pleased when you take a baby on an aeroplane. It gives them something genuine to do.'

'What did you mean when you said Don tries people out?' she asked at dinner. 'Sometimes I wonder if he'd really rather I was – No. What did you mean?' He realised she had been going to ask him something about sex, and he knew enough about Don's veiled temperament to be sure that he could have been no help to her at all.

'In the war he was like this with his platoon. He never said anything to them directly. They thought he was playing with them. They couldn't get into contact with them. He found out how they were by saying in a general way that all privates were lazy. If they were bloody minded after that, he knew they were ok. If they weren't, it meant they were too beat to care and he got them a rest. I suppose they knew it was better than a thump up the crutch. But it didn't stop them mistrusting him. It was all right for a time because they suddenly discovered he was frightened, which made them quite like him, but then he wrecked that by being more sardonic than ever because he was horrified that they knew it. In the end he behaved very well. That's Army for being brave.'

'He says you were.'

'I wasn't at all. I think the most difficult thing must have been to have been on a merchant convoy. I don't think I could have done that.'

They were offered soup, fish, veal cutlet, vegetables, strawberry yoghurt, cheese, and then a yellow ice-cream with fan-shaped wafers. She ate everything; she had thought it was all over with the cheese, and when the ice-cream came she looked enchanted.

What do you miss most?' he said.

'Pierozki,' she said at once.

They had three of the railway company's half bottles of wine, and then a glass of Calvados. She did drawings for him with a special black-ink pen on the back of the *wagon-restaurant's* plates.

'Have you ever seen Don with animals?' he said.

'No?'

'You know we share a place in the country. We've got horses and a few pigs and hens, and he has peacocks. And a dog. When there's anything wrong with them he's much better with them than I am. He should have been a vet.'

'A vet?' She laughed at him. 'What happens when he's up in London? Or in America? Or wherever else?'

They get ditched, of course. We have to cope, or a man comes in. You're quite right.'

She drank a great deal of Calvados and seemed elated. When they went back to this *wagon-lit* she asked the attendant if he could send a telegram from the frontier for her. The attendant looked mulish. 'Please,' she said.

'Perhaps he can't because we don't stop long enough,' said Harry. 'Or because there isn't anywhere to do it from.' He wished she would drop it; obviously it wasn't possible.

'I beg of you.' She was speaking in French. 'You could manage it, couldn't you? It's to my husband. I haven't seen him for eight years.' Eventually she found an Italian in the *wagon-restaurant* who was more sentimental and said he would do it.

47

'I didn't know you were married,' said Harry.

'My ex-husband. I had to say husband to get the man to do it.' Harry laughed at this, mostly at himself for being a little shocked at the fib, because he humbly accepted Don's jibe that his scruples were often due more to upbringing than to principle.

'Does he live in Rome?'

'Apparently. He suddenly wrote to me and asked if I ever came to Rome to work. I don't; I've come specially, but I'm not going to tell him that. He said he'd seen a drawing of mine. That's how he got in touch. He's never answered my letters but perhaps it was because he didn't get them. Anyway, he must feel differently now.' She seemed excited and confident.

'Is he Italian, then?'

'Andrzej?' She laughed. 'He was once the most Polish man you could think of. Then he turned into a Russian in a Polish skin, which was a useful sort of person to be in Warsaw under Stalin.'

'You're not walking into something? What sort of prize are you?'

'None. Since Stalin those dangers are different. Everything's different. Andrzej may be out of a job for all I know.'

'I didn't mean what sort of political prize. I hadn't even thought of that.'

'I'm certainly not a private prize. Is that what you meant? He doesn't love me at all. I'm a dead letter to him. Andrzej's Catholic. 'We didn't have a Catholic wedding and we're divorced, so the marriage never existed. When civil marriages are dead to a Catholic they never happened. Nothing remains. No souls, like cats. It will be good to see him again, that's all. I never thought I should. He didn't answer any of my letters, not ever, you see. I've said that before, haven't I? I'm sorry to be boring. Forgive me.' She was slightly drunk and unlike herself. 'Do you know that apart from the Polish bookshop this will be the first time I've talked Polish for four years?' She said a Polish tongue-twister very quickly. 'Then there's one in Czech. All consonants.' She said it. 'No vowels, you see. It's meant to show what a barbaric language it is.'

'It sounds exactly like the Polish one to me. You do harp on about the difference, don't you? I thought Central Europe was supposed to be less chauvinist than England. We'd better have some more to drink, hadn't we? Would that be a good idea?'

'The way you say that.' She was suddenly struck by him as if he had been lit up with a photographic flash, and memorised what he looked like. 'It's easier not to be nationalist when you've got the sea round you like England. Your frontiers don't move about. You can have your *entente* with France and not believe a word of it because you know you're quite safe from intrusion. Whereas if you'd been in the middle of Europe you'd probably have lost Surrey and Sussex to the French by now, and there'd be wine on the Pullmans and *pissoirs* in Godalming. Russians are always calling the Poles nationalist; I suppose they are. I mean I suppose we are.' She changed her voice. '"Nationalism is dead, my friends, meaningless, a habit of thinking. Then someone else says: "Yes: I agree that the existence of nations cannot be rationally justified. However."' She was imitating a roomful of drawling voices, dropping into a style of clever, watchful truckling that she hadn't heard since she left Poland, because the taste of Warsaw talk was suddenly lying on her tongue again.

He took her back to his *wagon-lit* with a bottle of Calvados and she had some more to drink. He kept up with her, because he thought it fair, perhaps, or because he dreaded losing her to alcohol and her past.

She was submerging more and more in both 'However, my friends, for the moment one has to deal with this undesirable illusion of nationalism as if it were a fact. For fact it is; *eta fakt*, as our sad brothers the Russians say. Russian is the most beautiful language in the world. Censorship must be harder for them to bear than anyone. Not to be able to say what they feel; no more outpouring of the soul, *izlivit dushu*. Poor sods, what do they pour their souls out in now? Music, I suppose. No more confessions by the samovar. The Russians turned the confession into an art form long before the purge trials or the couch were thought of. Their whole style of talking gone, that's what that means . . . Do you know that some lawyer who went to Russia some time or other to look at the Tsar's gaol found that more than three-quarters of the prisoners were there because they'd confessed? Of their own accord, for the sake of *izlivit dushu*. Do you think there'll be time for me to send Andrzej a telegram from Genoa to say I'm coming? Outpouring of the soul. It's rather a luxury, isn't it? To us. But for them not to be able to do it. Ah. Oh no. What a harness to clip them into. It must be like coming from the West Indies to an English winter on a gas ring. When I feel generous I think that it's probably easier for Poles to have to watch our mouths because we do it anyway. We don't mind shutting up, you see. The essence of the famous Polish irony is to shut up. Or do you say belt up? I never remember which class says which in England . . . Russians have always persecuted the Poles for being nationalistic. The discovery that a Polish Communist suffers for the plight of his country has always been enough to discredit him with the Russians. That's where Andrzej's so clever. You see, he never expects anything better. He has the enormous gift of cynicism. A Jesuit Marxist cynic is unbeatable. Yes? I don't suppose you know what I'm talking about. I'm sorry.'

'It sounds impossible, that's all.'

'It could only sound impossible to an Englishman. You have no idea, have you?' She grinned at him, with the hermetic patronage that he had noticed sometimes in the religious towards doctors in the presence of the dying, and if he hadn't been lulled with drink he would have been angry. He got up and went out into the corridor and thought she had gone to sleep, but she was weeping, and then asked if she could use the little basin in his compartment to brush her teeth.

'What a lot of gold teeth you've got,' he said. 'You must have been unwell. Was that because of the war?' He often said 'unwell' when other people might have said 'ill'; his patients noticed it. The word extended to them a sort of attention and gravity.

'I suppose it probably was.' At least she could still stop herself telling this detail of her past. She had been clamorous and detested herself for it. The taste of the menthol helped her to recover. She put her toothbrush and the tube of toothpaste back into her bag, and I then held out the tube to him. 'Would you like some?'

'I'd rather have another drink.'

'I must go.'

'When was the last time you saw him?'

'Literally the last time? I don't remember it very clearly.'

'Don't go. You're better now, aren't you?'

'The time that always seems like the last time was a day in Cracow, one morning just after the end of the war. The Red Army had been letting off rockets all over the place the night before and people got very drunk. I'd just watched everyone else. You won't believe it but I usually find it almost impossible to get drunk. The alcohol doesn't seem to take properly. Andrzej was trying to start a magazine. I was going to do drawings for it. The next morning we started work quite early. The window of the office looked onto the back of a rather beautiful old building that had been turned into a prison. The men in there were all very young and hanging out of the windows. It was sunny. They were trying to get warm. One of them was fishing for a bit of paper on the ground with a hook. He never managed to get it. I'd thrown it wrapped round a stone but the stone made it too heavy to pick up. Then I threw another one wirth a lighter stone but it didn't get there. It was only a joke to make him laugh. They were my friends, you see? And Andrzej's, supposed to be. They were partisans. But of course they'd learnt too much about fighting by then. It wasn't exactly that they had a taste for conspiracy, it was just that they wanted to drive out the Russians. They'd survived till 1944 and done what the Government-in-exile wanted and risen against the Nazis, and the Russians had just sat on the other side of the river and waited till they'd finished themselves. They were an awkward element, you see. They had to be what you call "contained", and the neatest way to contain any hero who's likely to turn into an enemy is to persuade him to kill himself off fast so you can say he'd have been on your side if he'd survived. The others were rounded up slowly. Some of them hung out in the woods. They had to be called enemies of democracy by Moscow trimmers like Andrzej. It's true that at the end of the war a lot of the people who could best put the country together were Communist. And some good artists in those days. And thoughtful people. I mean by that serious people, not trigger-happy, and not only authoritarians like Andrzej. Also a lot of opportunists and thugs, but I suppose they didn't do any better on that band-wagon than on any other. I was a Communist for a time. I suppose I'm still a sort of failed Marxist. It seemed the natural thing. We had to have a mechanism. But what about the people in gaol? Andrzej and I quarrelled until we had no taste for each other. It was the old one about means and ends. In that situation it's no help to you that it's been fought so many times by better and cleverer people. I couldn't remember anything they'd said, anyway. Though Andrzej seemed to be doing it out of the book. He was chain-smoking and had a hangover and he looked ill. The boy kept trying to hook the bit of paper. Andrzej could see it all and it didn't *bother* him, that was the point. In the end he told me to do a drawing of it and I suddenly knew he wouldn't publish it whatever happened, that he'd say he would and then lose it or burn it or even keep it in his wallet as a piece of evidence against me and never, never wonder about it. That's all, I think.'

He gave her another drink. 'I think we should have the bed half the night each. I really don't want you to go back to that second-class compartment of yours. Besides, you'd wake people up.' He expected that she would refuse, and he told her later that if she had done he would have given her up. To his pleasure she thanked him and went to sleep instantly.

He stood in the corridor and walked about, smoking gently and feeling surprisingly well. At five o'clock he woke her as he had promised, and slept himself till after ten. He found her again in the restaurant car.

'Do you feel bad?' he said.

'No. Very, very good. You've got a different tie on. Magenta. To be able to wear magenta with a hangover; that's mettlesome!'

'I suppose I'm really too old for it.'

'Bollocks. Too old to be Shirley Temple, too young to be Methuselah, too thin to be the fattest man in the world and the wrong sex to have a baby. Whatever are you talking about?'

'Well, it's true about the baby! Did you send your telegram?'

'From Genoa? Yes.'

'Why do you keep sending them?'

'I expect he doesn't really believe I'm coming. After all this time I wouldn't. Would you?'

He thought about it. 'Yes, I think so. Since it was you. I'd believe you'd do what you said. And surely he would, as a matter of temperament. From what you tell me he doesn't sound a very doubting man. It isn't easy to surprise a dialectician, is it?'

On the platform in Rome he gave her his telephone number and said he would be in by eleven that evening if she wanted to talk to anyone. He was unsure whether or not he was intruding.

'I behaved indecently last night,' she said. 'I'm so sorry,'
He didn't seem to mind.

V

Everything that night seemed upside down. Andrzej lived not in the poor flat that she had imagined, unconsciously fusing it with the one in Warsaw, but in a grand old house full of leather chairs and black Cretan bulls. Two impassive Great Danes sat behind the glass front door, and she took them at first to be marble. Andrzej spoke to her not in Polish but in English, with a heavy American accent. And he had a wife, whom it seemed necessary to pretend to have known of, a thin New England professor of Church History who was presently writing a book. Moreover the three of them turned out not to be alone, as she had thought, but fenced in with guests who made their way to the huge brown marble table of drinks without asking. It was she who was the acquaintance here, the outsider, the one-shot dud who would not be asked again. It was almost as if she had been invited from England to make up the numbers.

Andrzej's eyes looked alarming, like the end of potholes, and her immediate instinct was that he must have committed some crime. His adoption of America was ghostly. He even walked differently, with his pelvis tucked under him like a GI, and his phrases confused her. She had tried to kiss him at the door but he avoided it, shook hands, introduced his wife and asked if she would like to wash. But what he actually said was: 'Do you want to wash up?' And though it took only half a second for her to guess what he meant, she was so thrown by everything else that she embarked on an absurd explanation that in English this meant something different. 'I thought you meant . . . in England it means the plates. Wash the plates.'

'Oh,' said Dolly, his wife, 'do the *dishes*. How fascinating. Really.'

It was a poor interlude of misplaced comic business, like falling into the grave at a funeral.

After a time Kakia saw that he wasn't really Americanised after all. It was a very good performance, almost perfect, of quite a large number of parts in the Western alliance. This was not a matter of an adopted nationality; it was a pretence of a cultural position, shoring up what he had borrowed from America with West European bile and glee, and enlivening it sometimes for his own amusement with the whimsical persecutions of English public school men, or with anti-Americanism at its most ceremonious and slothful. The American at the dinner was treated as an exhibit, and he seemed to have been invited in order to hang himself. Andrzej sat in a leather chair the colour of ancient book-bindings and coaxed him to be foolish with a dreadful show of love, watching Kakia slyly for a sign of compliance.

'And this new movie is about violence?' he said.

'We rolled it as a story about what is indeed, what is the special problem and concern and the most urgent and pressing Nietzchean or Dostoevskyean fantasy of our time, which is. Uh. Violence. As you say and as better men than you or I have said many times. If you ask me our thinking on this, then I will tell you that I do not plan or presume to plan or pre-ordain that special order of experience which film director of his nature feels drawn to and which can become clear to us only when it has been regurgitated as it were in the process of editing. When I see it I shoot it and this is all I can tell you. Inasmuch as I may be said to be a creative artist I will take a decision mayhap about a particular style or mode of treatment or way of looking at the world that may suit or express or at any rate best complement the area of. Uh. Interest. In so far as we would have wished to deliberate upon our methods and approach we found what I could call an alcoholic manner. By this of course I do not mean that we ourselves were alcoholic. Nor indeed for that matter were our subjects. I speak only of the flavour, the special aura as it were, of our method of work, which we did not wish to be simplicistic but merely instinctual, which did not consist or subsist in what we were shooting but rather in the particular intoxication or epileptic rhythm of the processes by and through which we decided to shoot, in so far as it could be said that we ourselves were knowingly or consciously or even deliberately involved in these decisions.'

Andrzej filled up the director's whisky tumbler and fed him another question as if he were giving a bird a lump of sugar through the bars of a cage.

'In answer to your question, as of that time when I last saw the opera company you speak of, I thought or it seemed to me that this was a very, very interesting area of work. I would be glad to think that such a company could flourish or sustain itself in what I am bound to call the disaster area of Broadway.'

'Didn't you think it rather mandarin?' said Andrzej, in an accent that had now become almost totally English.

'What was that again?'

'Mandarin. Didn't you think?'

'I'd heard that too. That it was mannered', said Kakia quickly.

'It was certainly a very courteous occasion,' said the director, quite baffled. Andrzej looked as if he had won something. The director suddenly grew angry. He was not so thick that be was unaware of patronage and he tried to recover height by being criltical. 'Whereas this whole verse theatre thing you have in England is nothing. I tell you, it's nothing at all. Nothing but to empty the churches. If I may speak freely here, as I think I may, Andrzej. You try to go back and write blank verse at this point in time and where are you? I tell you where you are. You're a great preacher maybe but your religion isn't bringing them in any longer. This verse thing has been keeping them out for hundreds of years. You say it's art but I say it's *Tamburlaine* and I say to hell with it.'

Mortification had made him talk like a different sort of man and Kakia laughed, but it was an encouragement that he scorned. 'Warmed-over Marlowe; who wants it. Your average American in Europe goes to all the churches and galleries and old museums and he will gladly spend himself learning and gleaning what he may, and dipping into this pocket of his, that is always so very welcome, but there is a point beyond which even this willing student cannot be pushed. He is not without sense, I tell you, nor standards of his own, and some of the stuff he pays out to see will, as I say, contrive to drive him from his pew. I'm telling you, at *Hamlet* in Stratford-upon-Avon the audience were asleep, and most of them were Americans who had made reservation's for this play six months ahead and looked forward to it all their lives. At your Opera House in England, your *Royal* Opera House, they have sets that wouldn't be put on stage not *off-Broadway*, I tell you, Andrzej.'

'It's not my country,' said Andrzej. 'I agree with you all the way.' His accent had veered back again; it was now something mid-Atlantic, like an English late-night disc jockey's.

'And the orchestras! They play like as if they were telephoning it in. I tell you, they're going to live to regret it. The wool won't stay over your average American's eyes forever. I saw them in the orchestra reading *books* at Glyndebourne, during the performance. Writing letters. The whole percussion section was reading and writing letters. In the middle of an opera. *Paperbacks.* That's not what I came all that way for. I was in a box and I could see it all. I'm telling you, Andrzej, they're going to wish they'd never done that.'

At dinner Andrzej formally put Kakia on his right, with a look that was both a smirk and a shrug. He indulged his taste for the maliciously inopportune by talking to her loudly about their past in Poland, reminiscing in an apparently breezy way that must have been painfully exclusive to his wife. To Kakia it restored none of the assurance she pined for that he remembered the reality of either their life together or of their opinions. When she asked him what he was doing, he smiled and said that he was dabbling in a few things here and there because he had got tired of the drabness at home. It was the classic statement of the showpiece Communist abroad, made in the anointed tone of the man officially encouraged to reproduce the superciliousness of his enemies, and it gave Kakia a shot of pain even though she had prepared herself for something like it. The American director and the Englishman at the table seemed interested and impressed to watch him taking what they thought to be risks; the Italians took little notice.

'When people say that Eastern Europe's drab,' said the Englishman, 'aren't they reacting to the fact that there aren't any neon advertisements? Isn't that all it is? All visitors from the capitalist world always say this. It's the key word. Drab. Capitalists confuse salesmanship with liveliness.'

He was eager to recommend himself and to seem unguarded but the appeal misfired sorely, and Andrzej rejected the point for reasons as personal as the ones for which it was made.

I can't bear Poland at the moment,' he said. 'Besides, my lady wife had to have some shoes. Apparently Rome is full of shoes!'

'I thought you'd been in America. Can't she get them in America?' said Kakia.

'Her feet are an Italian shape, or so she tells me. When we were in America she didn't have too much time to shop. She was teaching pretty hard, you know. Well, I had to get her out of that. She taught a bigger class than I did.'

'They let you *teach*? Andrzej, how? How could you even get a visa?' She started to speak Polish.

'Dearest girl, we really mustn't be rude,' he said, and refused to do anything but smile and call her old-fashioned and doctrinaire. He was impossible to reach. Even his goosing attitude to his wife's work seemed a disguise. He affected a testiness and embarrassment about who was wearing the pants, but beneath there was an enormous and irreducible indifference. His personality seemed absent from everything he talked about. Where it was, perhaps not even he knew; it was squandered and she could find no trace of it.

'You have no idea of the manoeuvres', she said to the Englishman very fast. 'Unless you've lived there you can't know the battles that are fought. You're being very kind But how could you know? I don't know anyrthing about the pressures in England and I've lived there for years. You don't know what one pays for inventing codes, how a writer learns to communicate by tricks, how readers can fill in a gap if you plant it carefully enough. You can't guess the dissembling, and the cost of it. The cost is that when you've done it you're not the same.'

'You assume we don't understand,' said the Englishman. 'We're not without imagination, you know.' His mother, on the other side of the table, was trying her best to follow what they were talking about but most of it was going on on her deaf side and this made it no easier. It was her idea of a nightmare, this dinner party: nasty food, no laughs, the sort of talk you couldn't chip into; but Bertram was at his best and it was nice of him not to be ashamed of her. Every time he spoke it seemed to her that it was like another goal.

'The thing is, of course, Miss Grabowska,' he said; and Kakia said 'I'm called Gibbon now,' wishing she had had an opportunity to explain to Andrzej the gesture of giving up his name.

'The thing is that the Cold War has bitten into us so badly that we always underestimate the perception of the other side. Orwell's *1984*, for instance, when it gets through the lines, that always amazes people behind the Iron Curtain. They can't believe a Westerner could have had so much insight.'

'And, and. You, we, the Capitalist West, never believe that a Communist could have any insight about us. You missed out the difficult part, didn't you?' she said.

'I'll tell you one of the things I think about that,' said the Englishman. 'Not as a UN official, but as a private person who happens to have been recruited from England. It's all very well, but visiting Communists so often fix on the wrong things about England. Don't they? About mass media, for instance. They get serious about TV westerns, and thrillers, and hit-parade lyrics or whatever they're called, and seem to think they're significant because they're for the millions.'

'They are, and that's why,' said Andrzej.

'Yes and no.'

'Only Englishmen say yes and no like that.'

'It means no, I suppose, to be truthful. Is that what you meant? Anyway, what I was going to say was that it is frightfully crass really to make such heavy weather out of things like that. I see that in Russia they're serious. Or Poland. But not in England. Everyone *knows* that the popular stuff is rubbish. It's like – oh, bad food. Tinned food. Millions of people consume it and it doesn't make a ha'-porth of difference.'

'Bad food gives you rickets,' said Andrzej,

'Oh, come off it. England lives on it. I was brought up on tinned milk and baked beans.' His mother felt wretched; they had been poor but she had always done her best to feed him well.

'You surely know,' he went on, 'that when English people want to say anything important they simply don't *do* it in mass media. If it's any good it filters through to the big public through the press. If you really want to complain about the violence that's exhibited in English art forms you should look in the literary magazines. There's slaughter there and treachery and the Wars of the Roses every week. But Communist critics never take those seriously. They can't believe minorities are significant. So they go on grinding away about TV serials as if they've got some social importance. Really!' He lit a cigarette and felt he had betrayed his calling. 'You must remember that this is the result of a recent spell of home leave when I simply happened to entertain some Czechs and Hungarians whom I greatly respect and otherwise find very shrewd. It's not by any means the view of an international citizen.'

Andrzej was taking scarcely any food, no pasta or bread, hardly any wine. He was already a rake but he was frightened of getting fat. Kakia felt depressed by it. Not to gorge seemed the final refusal of sociability. What did it mean he was like in bed now? She speculated for a moment and loathed herself for it. An Italian maid cleared the plates away and Andrzej behaved to her rather disagreeably.

'The censors –' said the Englishman again. 'They seem – No I mean, what's the position about abstract art now?'

'Well, if you like abstract art,' said Andrzej.

The Englishman laughed nervously. 'I don't really. Not much. It's the principle, isn't it?'

'In Poland there are quite a lot of tinpot Picassos painting away. They don't represent anything important, in any case. I see no reason myself not to let people draw or paint whatever they want. It's journalism and fiction where a young society has to be careful. After all, you have your BBC code book, don't you? Your Lord Chamberlain and film censor and libel laws. Sometime soon you'll have commercial television and then there'll be a whole new set of pressures and proscriptions. And you have the voluntary censorship of a power-group of press lords who spend weekends with Winston or want an earldom.'

'I say. My goodness, you're well informed, aren't you?'

'He takes pride in not being foxed by art, you see,' said Kakia, turning her face to Andrzej so that she spoke about him but also to him. 'He's pleased that he saw through it so young. Whereas some people go on being gulled by literature all their lives.' She changed her tone and was able to address him directly. 'There's something very dangerous about all that which you can never see, can you? That it's possible that other people don't read or go the cinema or write or paint to show that they're right, but to find out whether. Who said that?'

'Brecht, I should think,' said Andrzej impeccably. She had forgotten to allow, as one does with lost intimates, that he had had years to learn other things. There was a silence.

'I've always been interested in politics ever since I was a girl,' said the Englishman's mother, who had had a working-class life and feared acutely having to speak up at gatherings like this. By the time she had nerved herself to do it the subject had generally moved on. She found it a little easier than usual this time because the host and his ex were obviously having words. 'I've always turned on the television for politics ever since I knew what it was. It's like religion, it probably is a warning to you.'

Andrzej looked at her son and moved his eyebrows drolly, but the man honourably responded to the gesture with contempt and Andrzej had to turn to the mother and say something.

'That's a good point about religion,' he said, finding he'd forgotten it already, amusing though it was.

'I don't think it would have been any better in Africa if Labour had been in, do you, dear?' she said to her son, whose official impartiality about English politics she never took seriously. She was Labour, but trying to be fair. 'We'd still have been in a mess but it would have been a rougher sort of mess.' She found it easier to talk in public if she fixed her eyes on him. 'If everything got nationalised at home I think I'd go out to sea and keep walking.'

At eleven exactly Kakia asked if she could telephone someone. Harry's number was written on a neat scrap of paper that he had torn off a letter, and she had kept it in an enamel cigarette case that Don had given her for Christmas. Harry picked up the telephone at once.

'I wasn't sure you'd be there.' She gagged with fright as she said it and found herself full of excitement.

'I thought perhaps you might want to telephone, so I came back early. Where are you?'

'At Andrzej's. It's not what I thought. I'm going to go soon. I'm obviously expected to leave first.'

'I'm Sorry.'

'It's nothing. I don't know why I should be disappointed. I think it was probably homesickness, and that's gone now in any case. He doesn't remind me of anywhere any longer. Was your meeting all right?'

'Not like last night. I suppose you wouldn't –'

'You wouldn't like to have breakfast tomorrow, would you?'

'I was going to say that, you see. Do you think that would be a good idea?'

VI

Next morning he was wearing a beautiful sand-coloured suit and a fine white cotton shirt with a burnt orange tie. The room was old-fashioned and congenial, with a faded purple chaise-longue and a flowered Victorian pitcher and washbowl. 'Don't you look pretty?' she said. 'What's the suit made of?'

'I think it's called raw silk. I don't know why, though.'

'It looks like rope. Spun rope.'

They had thick black coffee and croissants and plum jam, which he bad ordered at exactly the time he had asked her to come.

'How did you know the coffee wouldn't be cold by the time I got here?'

'You wouldn't have been late, would you? You're not usually, are you?' She shook her head, and then had to qualify it because he spent so much care on such replies himself. 'Not if it matters. I'm late for hairdressers sometimes. And I run trains very fine.' She had never met anyone before with scruples of this sort who hadn't struck her simply as a laborious person.

'How is it that you don't stoop?' he said. 'All the girls I know stoop. And walk slightly sideways when, they're with me in the street, with their shoulders practically grazing the wall. Why do they do that? They always just manage not to touch it. Like a dog running along a pavement with its nose on the ground. It never does seem to graze itself but it makes one anxious to watch it.'

'I should have thought I did stoop, with all this drawing. Don't I? Perhaps English girls get lopsided because they always carry handbags.'

'Don't you?'

'No. I use pockets. I hate bags.'

'Is it possible to manage without?'

'If you want to.'

'In the war in England all the girls I knew suddenly started wearing webbing belts that had zip pockets. I used to take out one girl after another when I was on leave and every blessed one had the things on. It was like taking out the army.'

'All Englishmen seem to like girls in big hats and pale blue and full skirts and what they call frocks.'

'I like what *you* look like. You look marvellous. Dashing, I suppose that's it. The thing I hate most is girls wearing trousers when they've got girls' legs and girls' bums. It's all right if they've got boys' legs, but then you don't look at them anyway.'

Both of them remembered instantly that his wife had been wearing jeans when Kakia met her, and Harry had to say something about it.

'Sal looks good in trousers, though. She's got the sort of thighs that look all right in anything. She looks rather beautiful in jodhpurs. When I proposed to her she was in jodhpurs. That sounds like a line from a good comedy to take her mother to.'

'Is she all right?'

'Oh yes. She's fine.' He paused. 'I think she's a bit bored. Perhaps she should try to get a job. But I don't know what. I can see it must be tiresome from her point of view.'

'What?'

'Doctoring. It doesn't interest her. Why should it? But it means we don't talk much, because she's rather a silent girl anyway. I never feel I'm a particularly good person for her to be living with.'

She waited and wondered whether she could ask why they had married each other but felt she must hold her tongue. He replied simply enough to what she hadn't said. 'I was billeted with her family. She was very unhappy. I suppose we got married partly because it seemed to make life easier for her. Her mother is an old cow. Sal was sent to boarding school when she was three to get her out of the way. *Three*. It was a very smart place and she learnt nothing at all. Then in the war the school started flogging the kids' food coupons and all they had was bread and potatoes and half a pint of milk a day. Whenever their parents were going to see them they were given roast beef and Yorkshire pudding the day before, because the headmaster reckoned children had got short memories and would talk of nothing else. Sal's mother didn't notice for years. The child got sores all over her. They've left scars that you can see still when she goes brown. The kids discovered that if they spat into a little bottle all day they could suck the spit in bed at night to stop hunger pains.'

Kakia looked out of the window and found nothing to say.

'I can't meet that woman,' he said. 'I can't be civil to her.'

'Where did you fight in the army?'

'Europe. Belgium mostly.'

'Was it bad?'

'It got worse when you hadn't slept. I thought I might stop being frightened soon but I never did. I used to sweat so much that my boots were like lakes. I longed for clean socks more than anything because I was afraid I stank. I change my socks now every time I get home. My old ma used to send me parcels of them. Socks and those bars of dried bananas. They were tobacco coloured, weren't they? and hard to chew. They looked like elephant shit but they were delicious. Did you have them? I'm sorry. I'm afraid people do this in England about the war. Nothing else seems to have happened much since. We had a Coronation and a Festival of Britain that were supposed to celebrate the new Elizabethan age, but they were more melancholy than anything else. They were like birthday parties that everyone had taken a lot of trouble over for you, but at a time when you simply didn't want to be reminded of yourself!'

'I was here,' she said.

'Of course you were. I'm sorry.'

'I drew people camping out in the Mall waiting for the Coronation. The place was full of Australians who didn't believe how cold it could be. They kept talking about Bondi Beach and barbecues. Do you know who Andrzej reminded me of? I hadn't thought of it before. He's a little like Don. He's less nice, of course. And not at all infectious or softhearted. I don't mean they're altogether alike. I can't imagine Andrzej getting stricken about people in pain. But he has the same thing of pretending he's not wretched when he is, and making calculations on the assumption that everyone else is as sophisticated as he is. Not everyone sees life as a series of bargaining points. He went for some Englishman's old mother last night because he thought she was being sly and anti-Communist when she was only trying to do her whack of the talking. Which was, I tell you, sticky. Vicious. And nothing was *said*. Nothing, nothing.'

Should we have some more coffee?' Harry said. 'Who was the Englishman?'.

'This is our second breakfast in succession. Do you realise. that? How good. He was in the UN, I think. He was trying to explain to Andrzej the way things are done in England. As though it was a sort of code that foreigners had to learn to crack, and as though it was going to be like that forever. The usual thing. There was something about TV not being significant because no one who knew anything about England would use a mass medium to say anything they seriously meant.'

'I wish I thought we were going to have breakfast together tomorrow.'

'When are you going back?'

'I'm going to America. I thought you knew. Didn't I say? For two months.' He poured more coffee. Because he had found it painful himself to say that he was going, he understood also that she felt inexpressibly crestfallen. 'This is where people usually say "Well, it's only two months, isn't it?" It's as long as the summer holiday when you're a child. As long as the thirty-second to the fortieth week of having a baby. That's a very long time.'

'Are babies what you do mostly?'

'I like obstetrics. I'm not sure that it counts as proper medicine really. The problems are easier. I mean the problems for someone with my temperament. I can't deal with people's despair. The brutality that doctors have, or need to have or fall into, I don't know which it is, but I can't bear it. 'When I was a student, one of the chiefs said on a ward-round to a woman who had cancer: 'Well, we'll soon have that breast off. You won't be needing it any longer, will you, because you've had your hot flushes.' Something like that. I think he meant it to amuse the students. Perhaps he was even trying to steal her. How can doctors stop themselves getting like that? I've never forgotten it.'

'What did you mean when you said obstetrics weren't proper medicine?'

'I mean that they're not firstly about disease. The atmosphere is different. It makes doctors react differently. When a gynaecologist does a Caesarean he doesn't take out a rotten appendix, he takes out a baby. An obstetrician is in an open situation with another human being, instead of a secret situation where he has to ignore the patient and address himself to an aberration. I'm not surprised such a lot of doctors behave like shits. It's because they spend their lives in a relationship that's practically unbearable.'

'I don't see that. A tumour is just as much a part of the patient as a baby. And why do doctors behave so possessively about it?

Those folders in English hospitals saying "Not to be handled by the patient." For god's sake, it's *your* illness. Not a piece of hospital property. You're the one who's going to die of it.'

There are reasons less disreputable than people suppose! It's not entirely black magic or paternalism. At least that's what they say. I suppose the truth is that I don't agree or else I should be a more successful doctor. I'm too irresolute to be altogether good at it.'

'You? Oh no.'

'You might say that the real trouble is the hierarchy. That if the whole of medicine weren't such a caste system, with consultants bawling out senior registrars for bothering them or alternatively for not telling them something, and senior registrars hating the housemen for not giving them enough time to study to be consultants, and housemen getting five hours sleep in a hundred-and-eleven hours of duty, and sisters being grand to student nurses, and all nurses being treated like Victorian between-maids by the consultants, and no one in the whole bang shooting-match ever, ever letting anyone more junior in on his blunders – that if it weren't all like this, then the patient wouldn't be the untouchable at the bottom of the heap. As a layman you might easily say this.' She waited for his rebuttal. 'And if you did I think I would agree.'

'What do you say when people ask if they're going to die?'

'They don't, pray heaven. Hardly ever. When patients are very ill there's a sort of agreement between you about it. I don't have to deal with it very often now. When they ask, I tell them but those people know already. When they don't ask, I watch them, and I've never been aware that anyone was deceived. I think I would know. I've always been quite sure that they knew; or at any rate that the necessary part of them knew.'

'What does that mean?'

'I mean the only part of oneself that is at all capable of facing dying, the unconscious self that isn't in communication with other people. Because it exists in isolation, it finds the idea a little more possible; that's all. It's a cruel thing to ask of the conscious mind. Relatives often find it intolerable to watch, the simultaneous knowing and not knowing. And not easy to believe in. They're tormented by drugs that drag out life and they abuse us for using them. I'm not sure. Someone will often die with less terror after a long illness than if you'd had to let him go at once. After a time there's something that gets used to the idea. It's what's called a merciful process. And I hate it with all my heart, that's the truth of it. When I die, I hope I die in fury. Oh my dear Kakia, why did you ask me this? It's what I do obstetrics to avoid. I'm a very cowardly man.'

VII

From Chicago he sent her a postcard:

'What a good thing you were on that train. I'm reading a load of rubbishy women's magazines that I bought at London Airport. They're full of what they call girl-talk here and v. good for homesickness though I have to hide them from the learned men who come into my room for highballs. Hope you're all right and not brooding about that dinner. H.C.'

His writing was very clear, but all the same he wrote her name and address in capital letters as if the card might well not get to her. A month later she had another one, from Boston:

'Boston v. beautiful. The hospitals are amazing. Posh families here think they have a BRITISH ACCENT (means English, not Welsh or New Zealand). Crackers, of course. The cupola of Mary Baker Eddy's Church is glaring into my room and rebuking me for false belief in medicine and mortal mind. It's called the Mother Church, which is all right if you like your mother I suppose. England from the papers sounds a bit tetchy and fed up. Are you all right? H.C.'

She was living in Broad Court in an attic studio that she had white-washed and stripped herself. At night she could see the audience strolling inside the foyer of the Opera House in the intervals, and the light from the globes outside Bow Street police court. She had given up the magazine job and was washing-up now in a restaurant at night so that she could draw in daylight. Occasionally what she did was published, but only if it happened to have someone well-known in it. No one was at all interested in drawings of what she saw in England. Several publishers looked at a dummy she did of a book, but said it would only be viable commercially if she had a name. London seemed to be full of competent artists begging famous people for sittings so that they had something saleable to flog; they were a craven tribe and she drew them as bad-tempered, ageing foetuses to keep her spirits up.

Don liked the Broad Court attic and came round often after she'd finished work in the restaurant. He lived permanently in a hotel. She asked him why, and he said it went with preferring to eat in a restaurant instead of in people's houses. And why this? 'Choice' he said instantly. He pecked at his cigarette and looked fierce and comic as he always did when he was about to define something, whether it was about himself or anything else. 'I like to have a menu. Ideally everyone would have a menu for every decision in their lives. A restaurant is a brothel where you are free to choose the girl. Food in houses is bourgeois monogamy.' This would have been more convincing if he had ever chosen anything in a restaurant except the same *prosciutto* and *steak tartare*, fancying the idea of himself as a man who liked his meats raw, or if he had been in the slightest inclined to go into a brothel instead of much preferring the company of girls whom he could have debates with. The adjective 'bourgeois' told Kakia that he was flirting with her politics again. He was magnetised by the sheer explanatoriness of Marxism, even though he was dazzled by America, and sometimes he seemed to get a jab of erotic excitement from the mere fact of her nationality. He was always fencing with her to make her state her position and pestered her to name her politics as if he were hunting for the identity of a lover whom he would have been obscurely relieved to discover. She complied with his catechisms only because they were easier and less painful to him than his struggles to make love. That autumn she had a recurrence of asthma, which she hadn't suffered from since she was a child, and it extinguished her own sexual initiative like a bucket of sand. Don would often stay very late and make her a cup of soup while she wheezed and took pills and lay down on the sofa under a beautiful Chinese blanket that he had bought for her. It was orange on one side and magenta the other and bound with bright green satin ribbon. She propped up Harry's postcards against the base of a lamp, mostly because she liked looking at them but partly in the hope that Don would see them so that he was informed of them without her having to bring them up. When he had stayed too long he would often yawn secretly every now and then for an hour or more, the lower part of his face lengthening suddenly so that he looked like a horse.

'Harry's in Boston,' he said one night. She had no idea whether or not this was to imply that he now realised she knew it. It might equally well be to test her and see if she would volunteer it. For some reason she was damned if she was going to surrender her privacy to the extent of spelling out that she had had two postcards from him. Don lived a game of innuendo that intrigued only him, and in stronger moods she declined to play it.

'Boston is one of the few American cities that regrets the past,' he said. 'That's why I like practically anywhere else in America better. Boston's like England. Up to its ears in yellowing photographs. Everyone in England seems to spend their time wishing they were still Edwardian, or still Victorian, or that we still had India, or that they were one of the few, or that Fabian Socialism still worked, or that Chatsworth had never been opened to the public, or that trades unions weren't so Tory.

Why's he gone there? I suppose you could say that Harry was the natural Bostonian of obstetrics.' He was doing this to goad her into revelations because she generally challenged him about his aphorisms when they were especially meaningless, but tonight she disappointed him. She felt ill and light, and as if the skin on her skull had been anaesthetised; she kept rubbing it back to life.

'People in England often make jokes that seem very serious about this,' she said. 'About the way you all long for the war. They talk about having to find a moral equivalent of the stimulus of the Battle of Britain. But the real problem is different now, isn't it? That was the situation after the *first* world war. The really pressing thing for well fed countries is to find a moral equivalent of poverty, isn't it? This is what flash left-wing Tories like you are really on about when you gripe about steel workers getting twenty quid a week and going to sleep in front of a telly that they've bought on the HP or having a holiday on the Costa Brava. You're not really cross that the man's going to have a holiday, you're cheated that he doesn't need you any longer. Nothing to do for him that's nice and simple, like clearing him out of a slum. No one in English politics has found an appeal that has anything like the poetic meaning and urgency of a lot of one's compatriots suffering. The Socialists certainly haven't. It's considered rather tasteless for a Socialist to recognise that the hunger marches are over. I'm not wrong, am I? When someone uncovers a good Dickensian scandal, like the Church Commissioners making a pile out of a tenement, there's an enormous secret gratitude for a good clean problem to put right again.'

'You're saying exactly what I said. That England hankers after the past. That's why I like America. I told you.'

'Oh, don't be *silly.* What's the difference over that between the two?'

'Only a foreigner could ask that.'

'America's submerged in the present but that isn't the point. The essence is that neither of you have got a sense of the future. All the hankering after the past here is a metaphor for something else – for having no vision of a future that is at all exciting to anyone. A whole dimension of historical consciousness in people has simply been cut off. There's no Utopia any longer. The future is something that just happens here. It hasn't been imagined. England and America know that they've had revolutions but no one feels that there have been any revolutionists. That's the most painful humiliation in social history. We're living in highly educated idealistic societies that haven't thought or planned or dreamed of anything that's happening to them. Why do you think everyone hates technology except technologists? Because they didn't conceive of it. It never took place in their imaginations. This is something special to you. Victorians lived in the future all the time. So do people in Communist countries now.'

'Of course. Because there's nothing else for Communists to do. Everything in the present is too disappointing to think about. And oh, how monstrously those pipe dreams are going to be betrayed.'

'Probably. But you would be right to bear these people in mind. They do exist. Millions of people whose imaginative life is as different from yours as an Elizabethan's would be. They are at least an assertion that a sense of creating one's own future is still possible. That it isn't extinct in a time of cybernetics.'

'Dogmatic optimism isn't an imaginative life.'

'You underestimate it. It has more personal reality to some people than you think.'

'Are you a Communist?'

'You do want an answer to that one, don't you? No. I've never struggled to explain myself to you because all the things I could tell you would have the wrong meaning for you anyway.'

'I suppose you've talked to Harry about it?'

'Not much'

'Why haven't you talked to him about it? Don't you like him?'

'You know I do.'

'Well then, why haven't you told him? Hasn't he asked you?'

'Why should be?'

'He must have asked you.'

'I may have talked about it. I can't remember. It's a question that's too complicated to answer if you put me up against a wall. And too simple to ask. It's not the sort of question he would ever put. Is it?'

'What do you mean?'

'He just observes.'

'What do you mean?'

'Over things like this he just watches. He's a doctor.'

'You mean you think I'm curious.'

'Don't play. Please.'

'You mean I'm bothering you. You don't trust me.'

'For Christ's sake.'

'What did you mean when you said Harry just watches?

Can't you talk to each other? I always imagine you talking endlessly.'

'We've only met twice. You always get me to say what you want in the end, don't you?'

'Why don't you like me asking about him? Doesn't Sal know? Is that why you don't like me asking?'

'Of course it isn't. I haven't the faintest idea if she knows or not. There's nothing for her to know. Why do you do this?'

'I don't know what you mean. I'm in love with you.'

'You make yourself wretched. By sparring and pestering.' But she was quite wrong about this; he was buoyant.

'Will you make me some soup?' she said.

'You're not feeling well.' He altered at once. While he was in the kitchen she got up and fetched Harry's postcards and sat with them in her lap. They were the trophies that Don wanted from her: not only a sight of them, but offered to him by her; and he had manoeuvred a situation where it would now seem more significant if she were apparently keeping them from him than if she shook them in his face. She held them out when he came back with the soup. And then he surprised her, as he sometimes did. He was suddenly confident with her and tender, and the sight of the cards no longer seemed to be a prize. He looked at them quickly and said nothing, dismissing them practically rudely. He had given himself some soup as well, and dropped into it a cold potato and a piece of ham that he had found in the fridge. It was two in the morning and his skin was opaque with fatigue.

'Shouldn't you go home?' she said. 'What does Harry mean there about mothers? Does he hate his?'

'You're ill, aren't you?'

'No, this passes! I just have to wait. But I would rather like to go to bed.'

'He manages her all right. Hasn't he told you?'

'We don't know each other at all. You don't seem to believe us.'

She had said 'us': the mixture of release and dread that he felt at hearing the word was so afflicting that he forced himself into another topic. This was part of his quality; though he was impatient with the difficulties of others he was far more ruthless towards his own. Kakia sometimes felt grateful that, however hard a time she might happen to be having with him, at least it was softer than the one he gave himself.

'Did your parents look like you?' he said.

'Not at all.'

"You don't talk about them. Didn't you like them?"

'I draw them.'

'I didn't know that.' She made the sort of effort he would have demanded of himself, which was always to overcome lassitude. He feared failures of energy as other people fear the spectacle of temper or drunkenness. It was like the sun cooling, the end.

He spent a long time looking at her drawings. She was too exhausted and too remote from them to explain them, but she realised that he was mistaking their identities.

'Your father's very like you,' he said at last. 'Who's the other man? The one who looks like a diplomat?'

'That's the one who was my father. The other one was my mother's first husband. He happens to look like me but he was no relation at all. He feels to me the only kin I have and I never even knew him. I think it's just the upper lip that makes me look like him.' She roused herself and got a pill.

'What's that?'

'A sleeping pill.'

'Do you want me to go?'

'It's all right. Sometimes they make it easier to breathe.'

'Shouldn't you have a doctor.'

'It goes. At the end of the evening I sometimes don't seem to be getting enough oxygen out of the air. It's like having a drink and knowing there's water in the vodka,'

'Who was he?'

'My mother married him when she was seventeen. She was in France during the Great War. He was a French schoolmaster when they got married. I've always hoped to find someone he taught. I only know about him from my mother and she noticed so little. She had a bundle of his letters in the loft of our country house and she showed them to me once. She never even noticed that I kept them. They were wrapped up carefully in brown paper. She must have cared for them once, but I know she can't have looked at them often because some of the things she told me about him were wrong. They didn't agree with what he wrote to her. And the letters were kept in the wrong order and some of them were in the wrong envelopes. I've put them right. It took me a long time because he often didn't put the date on the letters and I had to work it out from the sense. He was shot.'

'Which battle?'

'He was a deserter. He was a *poilu* in the mutiny. For a schoolmaster to mutiny: he must have been hard driven. I suppose you know about the mutiny. Perhaps you don't. I believe it was hushed up. I think Haig knew about it, but Pétain asked him to keep silent. In 1917 nearly the whole of the French army mutinied. My mother was ashamed of it and told me Jean was shot because he was a German spy. I'm sure he wasn't. I've read his letters very carefully. He was an anarchist when he was a young man. In those days he lived in an attic with a lot of cats. He adored cats. His sketches are crawling with them, like Bonnard. He did a lot of sketches, rather bad, but my mother lost those. I saw them when I was small in the country and when I asked her for them she said she'd lost them. But I remember them quite well. There was an iron bed in a lot of them that looked like a bird cage, in a room with a sloping roof, and cats sitting on a beautiful girl's shoulder. I'm not sure if it was my mother: I think not. She wouldn't talk about him. He wanted to make films before he married her. He was a photographer's assistant in the evenings before the war and he borrowed one of the first movie cameras they had. He wrote to my mother about that. All the technical things that she wasn't interested in, of course. Once he must have gone to Nice and seen a funeral. It had to go round the back way so that the tourists in the grand hotels wouldn't see it and be put off their holidays. He scribbled some notes for a scene about that. It begins a film about a croquet tournament that gets broken up by some poor children pinching the balls and playing a game of their own. The notes were to himself and I couldn't quite imagine them, but in a letter to my mother he tried to describe the film to her. It was about revolution I think, or children's liberty. The children took over the structure of the game and turned it into one of their own. The people who'd been shielded from the sight of a funeral couldn't quite cope with them because the kids were quicker and had more sense of fun. From his descriptions the point might have been clumsy, perhaps. I don't know. You can't ask people to account for themselves. He should have been able to make his film, that's all. Perhaps it would have been extraordinary. I think it might.'

The sleeping pill was isolating her.

'Then my mother said she would marry him and he took a job as a schoolmaster because he needed some money to keep them both. After that the letters stop until 1916; I don't know why, because my mother said he was in several battles that were in 1915. He always refused a commission. The French Army was desperate for officers but he wouldn't do it. In 1917 after the Revolution in Russia the troops started singing the Internationale and forming Soviets, and an officer was so horrified that he fainted when he was addressing them. Jean helped to carry him out of the mud. It seems he did it very maliciously. I think he got a couple of his friends to carry the man like a butler's salver. That's the way he drew it. The letters are full of drawings.'

'Could I see them?'

'No, I don't think so. They were my mother's. I don't think he meant them for people to see. I shouldn't have seen the synopsis of his film. He should just have made it, that's all.'

'By now they're public property,' he said. She didn't listen to him.

'All April there had been rain and sleet. Officers were standing around in the Palace of Compiègne at the top of a marble staircase tapping the barometer. The weather never changed. They attacked because an ambitious general had decided to, but it was hopeless. Jean encouraged the troops to get drunk. They'd had no leave and every time they were promised a week in Paris they were only moved back to some sopping tents and told to go back to the front again twenty-four hours later. None of Jean's friends were left alive. All the men with him were strangers. When they attacked half of them were killed by their own machine-guns because they were firing short. Jean said the carcases swelled like horses. Someone coming back from leave brought him a cartoon from a Paris newspaper which had a happy-looking poilu with a pipe in his mouth and a rifle under his arm vaulting over trenches full of German corpses. When I read that I knew I wanted to draw. By the time the men left alive were drunk enough and despairing enough the mutiny spread. There were too many to shoot in the end, of course. They had to take hostages. They took a corporal from Jean's lot and shot him. It seems he was the best corporal. The colonel had been on leave and when he came back and they told him he wept. Jean had liked him.

What made him angry was that everyone assumed the mutiny was a German fifth column movement. It doesn't sound as if it had very much to do with Germany.'

'What was his surname?'

'I never saw it spelt.

Boileau, I think.'

'If your mother wouldn't tell you about him, how do you know he was shot?'

'She told me that. Over and over again, as if she'd been cheated by it. She was outraged. At the time I suppose she must have been unhappy but I couldn't find a trace of it left in her. I used to read the letters and wonder what she had been like when he wrote them. He doted on her and he knew that the situation he was involved in would offend her. I think she must have had very simple ideas about authority. When I knew her she was still very beautiful. On my birthday I was allowed to choose what she wore and I'd go into her bedroom the day before and arrange her clothes in the wardrobe and look at her shoes. The dresses were made of chiffon and silk and crepe de chine, and her evening shoes had buckles on them and glass ornaments. On one of them there was a huge pair of Georgian paste brooches. My father was very rich. They weren't especially fond of each other but I suppose it was as much as they asked. I think my mother must have tracked him down and married him in a mood of pure fury: fury with the war, and Germany, and soldiers, and most of all with Jean for getting killed for reasons that had nothing to do with her.'

'Aren't you being possessive about him?'

'Probably. I could only reconstruct him from the snapshots, and then years later I found a very clear photograph of him in some archives. Someone before the war had collected a lot of material. They must have been going to write a book.'

'Where is it all?'

'It might be anywhere now. Did you know that we reconstructed the Old Town in Warsaw? After the war we rebuilt it exactly as it used to be. From photographs and from Canaletto's paintings of it. Canaletto went there. Did you know that? What he painted was more help than the photographs. The paintings made it possible to re-build because the houses in them still seemed to exist. The photographs made them look extinct.'

'Where is the material about Jean?'

'I don't know. On Sundays my father used to take me into a park in Warsaw. There was a lake and a beautiful old house with a marble hall and women selling little parasols made of pleated paper. Before we went in we used to buy a bag of cherries off a stall in the road. One day it was the anniversary of the day Jean was shot, June 12th. My mother had stayed in bed and I thought perhaps it was because she was remembering it. Every year I'd never been sure whether she did or not. I wondered whether to save the cherries for her but she didn't like eating much except at meals. When we got back I went into her bedroom to see her and I expected the curtains to be drawn and her to be lying there perhaps, but she was dressed and learning Italian in an armchair and as jolly as a bee. I think she thought I had a headache or something.'

'Would you like to come to Poland with me and find all that stuff?'

Out of the careless coma of the sleeping pill she saw his meaning at last and realised that he was planning a television programme. The idea was one of such vulgarity to her that they quarrelled.

'Don't harangue me about it, that's all,' she said after a time. 'If you want to get anywhere you'll have to let me get used to it. At the minute I feel as if I've found you under a stone.'

'You're producing the classical response of the liberal bourgeois about a question of personal privilege.'

'Stop addressing me.'

'When it comes to the crunch, personal privacy is hallowed and the common interest goes to the wall.'

'I'm not the liberal bourgeois. Or *the* anything. I'm *a*, with *a* life that you suddenly want to commandeer, on a night when I've taken a sleeping pill and meandered stupidly in a way I'd never have done ordinarily. I was talking to myself. You were an eavesdropper.'

'You're the usual protesting radical discovered in the standard position of instinctive anti-radicalism.'

'Barging in isn't radicalism. You're passing off brutality as fearlessness. People often do.'

'Brutal only to your proprietary feelings.'

'Do you know why I'm angry? Because you appropriate, You treat everything as grist.'

At the same time she also understood that he was behaving airily to protect himself against some inadmissible wound that she had dealt him, and that the wound could only be sexual or to do with his pride in Harry. She roused herself to get up and go over to him. The asthma made her feel as if she were suffocating in feathers.

'Perhaps you could do it. Tomorrow I'll muster myself. You could certainly do it better than anyone else I can think of.

Tomorrow perhaps I'll respond more generously. You didn't ask very aptly, did you? The way I react would depend how and why.'

'I'm only concerned with *what*. Your questions aren't important,' he said, pecking like a bird at a cigarette.

'They're the only ones that matter in the slightest,' she said. 'I don't want some glib English television programme turning him into an anecdote. He wasn't one of your bloody little men,'

Part Two

VIII

'I wish to goodness he'd never got enamoured of peacocks, that's all,' said Harry.

'It's ridiculous getting worn out every weekend just because eight peacocks are feeling randy,' said Kakia.

'Will you feed them or shall I?' he said, sitting himself on a high kitchen stool and looking at the top of it warily first in case it should spoil his new country trousers,

'That means will I,' Kakia put down the pot she was stirring. 'I haven't slept properly since Thursday night in London. Their racket's more tiring than sex. How long does a peacock's season go on?'

'Two months, I think.'

'Is it the same noise all the time?'

'I don't understand it!'

'You didn't notice it last year, did you?'

'No, but we were away, weren't we?'

'I think Don must have some trick with them. I seem to remember he put them in the dark.'

'Where?'

'Perhaps in the potting shed.'

It was 1957. Harry and Kakia had been living together for two years. Don, as they kept saying to one another, had been very good to them. He had made scarcely any capital out of the situation. But there was no need to, of course, because it was made for him by the other two on his behalf. The country cottage was half his, but he always asked himself down as if he were a guest and seemed to regard his lost animals as part of the price that failure in love had exacted from him. Harry and Kakia found the position perplexing and were never sure if they were legatees or caretakers. Tonight they tried rounding up the peacocks and putting them in the potting shed, but the birds roosted in the fir trees and howled lecherously. After an hour in the dusk they caught two of them and shut them in but they were hen birds and the cocks only bawled to them more urgently than ever. So Harry let them out again.

'We might as well stop,' he said. 'This is about the time they stop a bit anyway, isn't it? And it's not very good for my trousers.'

'Perhaps if we went to bed at nine, as soon as it gets dark. If we kept their hours then we'd get the same amount of sleep as them.'

'What time was it when they woke up this morning?'

'Ten past four. They see the dawn. If only England didn't have this summertime thing we'd get another hour's sleep, wouldn't we?'

'No, an hour's less, surely?'

'What's putting the clock back for?' said Kakia after a pause. 'We had double summertime in the war.'

'But why?'

'I think it was something to do with the cows.'

'Well, it's got nothing to do with peacocks.'

The telephone went. Harry heard gratefully that it wasn't for him and meanwhile changed out of his new country trousers, which were not really very suited to the outdoors, into a pair of thigh-length waders that Kakia liked him in. He intended to black out the dog's shed. The peacocks seemed to enjoy themselves in there, eating their grain delicately in the presence of Don's borzoi and then courting in the straw. This was the root of the sleep trouble since the shed was immediately under Harry's and Kakia's bedroom window.

'It can't be good for the dog, either,' he said, passing through the kitchen on his way to the dogshed with a bundle of old bedspreads and his old khaki overcoat from the Army.

'You do look nice,' she said about the waders, stopping slicing to look at them.

'Who was it on the phone?'

'What are you going to do?'

'Black the buggers out. It wasn't Don, was it?'

'He wants to come down.'

'From New York?'

'He's flying back and wants to come straight down from the airport. He wants to bring Christabel,'

'Oh no.'

'She may be all right.'

'Not very likely.'

After he had been away a while she went out herself to shut up Don's ornamental ducks and feed his horse. Harry's horse was kept out to grass but Don's was a thoroughbred and there was a quite definable aura of ethics attached to the point of stabling it. Stabling meant feeding it, which was no burden, and exercising it, which was. Today they had put off everything, but tomorrow one of them was going to have to take the edge off the creature in case Don wanted to ride it and found them out. Kakia patted its incomparable neck boldly and gave it a sleeping pill to sedate it for tomorrow morning. The garden looked blue-green and lucid in the dusk and the white roses had acquired the strange primness of flowers at night. The noise from the peacocks was like the tearing of sail canvas. She realised that it must be because the electric light was on in the dog's shed, and went in to see. Harry was sitting on a crate opposite the borzoi. As usual she found the sight of him astonishing, a gift, like the spectacle of intuition or mercy. He was looking carefully at the dog, which had its head propped up on something under its straw so that it seemed rapt. The peacocks plainly found the electric light exciting. Half the window was blacked out.

'I was coming to get the ladder,' he said. 'And then I wondered if we shouldn't encourage them to wear themselves out so that they're quiet when Don comes.'

'Well, if they're not he'll know what to do with them, won't he?'

'It would be nicer to have seemed to have managed it, though.'

'Are you nervous?'

'It seems pretty tactless, doesn't it? To have a chap down to his own house where his best friend is knocking it off with his old girlfriend and you can't hear yourself think for the noise of peacocks' rumbo. I'm thinking of myself really. It will make me feel so unfeeling.'

The peacocks were at it all day next day, but more faintly, because Harry scattered their grain in a distant field where it took them some time to find the seeds in the long grass. In the night they had got restive in the dog's shed and by six in the morning they sounded as if they were plotting something occult. Kakia slipped out of bed then to exercise Don's horse so as to let Harry off having to do it, for though he was a much better rider than she was he was also more exhausted today. Harry thought she was in the lavatory and got up secretively to do the exercising himself; when she came back an hour and a half later he was still sitting on a stone by the loose box. She was leading the horse by the reins.

'What happened?' he said.

'It's all right. I just couldn't stick it up there any longer so I got off. The only way I could stop it bolting was by slanting it at a hill. I couldn't get its head round more than half-way and then it galloped itself silly diagonally. I thought it would be quiet this morning. How long does a Tuinal last?'

'You didn't give him a Tuinal?'

'Yes.'

'What, only one? You have to work it out by body weight. One would have been about as much good as trying to calm Medea down with an aspirin.'

'Oh.'

'When did you give it to him?'

'Late last night.'

'How many grains?'

'One of the big bombs in the top drawer.'

'They can elate, of course. If you fight the effect they can have the opposite effect from sedating.'

'I think that's what must have happened.' She watched the horse with loathing. 'Look at it. It looks radiant. I don't think it's been ridden all week. I believe AIf makes excuses to get out of it. He shows off about riding the thing but I don't think he likes it any better than I do.'

'He said his nerves played him up this week because of the peacocks. He hasn't done the lawn either.'

'He tried to get Mrs Everett to ring the vet about them. I found a note in the kitchen.'

'Why did he ask Mrs Everet to do it?' he said.

'She's supposed to know about animals, isn't she? Being a countrywoman.'

'Just because people have lived in the country all their lives it doesn't mean they're practical about it. Half the people in this village behave like Druids. I told her Don's coming. She's making the bed up.'

'Did you tell her Christabel was coming too?'

'Yes. She doesn't like her at all. Christabel fancies herself for having the common touch but she makes it very clear how common it is. I told Mrs Everett we had to have a go because of Don.

Christabel arrived in a fur-lined pea-jacket and a motoring veil, driving an open car with Don cold and grey beside her, looking after a small whirling animal that looked to Kakia like a mechanised pipe cleaner.

'What's that?' said Harry.

'It's Christabel's bush-baby,' said Don, scarcely able to speak for fatigue after the journey from New York.

After a short time in the very small sitting-room it was plain that Christabel had no idea what to do with the animal. Christabel was a famous and beautiful actress of thirty-five who collected worshippers easily, and she made it vaguely clear that at home there were always people who were wonderful with the funny rascal.

'It's not really very like a baby, is it?' said Kakia. It's more like a spiteful pullet.'

'He's terribly suggestible to atmosphere,' said Christabel. 'He simply *knows* that he's somewhere new and exciting where wonderful people live. I can't tell you how much more merry he is than in my dressing-room.' Christabel was famous for the way she enjoyed life. Her pleasure in what she called 'the good things' – which included Don, for the moment, and red wine, log fires, the natural childbirth trust, couture clothes and the long-suffering ally whom he called 'my faithful dresser' – was accepted by most people apart from the camp and the rude as being genuine. He had an unclouded nature, she felt, and if any barometer had ever dared to tell her anything else she would perhaps only have broken it. Some of the people who had close contact with her – her directors, for instance, her lovers, and the faithful dresser – found her unbounded capacity to enter into things disturbing. What was chiefly being entered into, they felt, was themselves, much as if they were being forcibly requisitioned and occupied. The wretched junk of their own personalities was being moved out to make room for the props of Christabel's glowing life, with the added irritation that they were prevented even from satisfactory surliness about it because of her impossibly unsullied tolerance of their defects.

Don had met her first in New York, where she had been a modest guest at the Actor's studio and discovered Zen. It was the perfect philosophy for her. Zen gave this unimaginative woman the style of shrewdness for the first time in her life. It also allowed her to quote sayings and tales that had the form of jokes without actually being funny, which suited her attitude to humour. Laughter irritated her. If other people joked too much her perfect eyes would glaze and cross slightly, as if there were a fly buzzing a little too close to the bridge of her nose for her to be able to see it. She was bilingual in Italian, and had borne a son in Rome at seventeen whose upbringing had caused her less trouble than any child anyone knew. She liked to astonish people by saying that he was grown up and at university. Her happiness with herself was so inviolate that instead of fearing that she would make herself seem older by the admission of an adult child she only made others feel callow, and as if her son had probably been born without pain out of her thigh.

'Do you know what I'm going to do next?' she said. 'With my darling Don. It's his idea. It's so *absolutely* – right.'

'No. What?' said Harry.

'You've got to guess,' she said. 'Kakia scraped the bushbaby off the curtains and said: 'A play at the Royal Court,' thinking that this was surely the next benison Christabel was liable to bestow.

'I'm not provincial enough for that, am I, darling? Dreary old cosmopolitans like me – Don?'

'Christabel feels all that raging social realism is rather vieux jeu.'

'You make me sound horribly crushing, darling. That's your voice saying that, isn't it? Not very generous. I think it's wonderful that it should be happening in England at last. One's been waiting for it for so many years. Our Odets period.' She had had tea with Clifford Odets in New York and told him all about it, and he had been so interested. She had seen Marilyn Monroe at the Actor's Studio, who was quite a charming girl.

She had just spent the weekend with the Barraults who had taken her to see Samuel Beckett's place for writing in the country; only a few bare walls and a stone floor, and they hadn't gone when he was there, of course, because he was such a recluse; but he was going to write a silent film for her, very modest, only a quarter of an hour. Harry disbelieved her and watched Don, trying to see how much substance there was to his apparent pride in her. He couldn't perceive whether she was simply a show-business trophy to him or perhaps even someone who had been blunderingly good to him. In public she had no more regard for him than for the bushbaby; but perhaps her iron-clad drive soothed him at the moment.

'You've simply got to guess. About this plan of ours: she said, putting her beautiful legs on to the hearth and sliding down onto her shoulder blades. 'The Royal Court wasn't even warm.'

'An opera,' said Harry obligingly.

'Getting hotter.'

'A musical.'

'*Harry*. You're uncanny. That's female intuition.'

'I'm a bit bent, I think,' said Harry cheerfully.

'What a dreadful thing to say. Poor Kakia.'

'Oh, I like it,' said Kakia, thinking she couldn't be serious. 'Bent does mean queer, doesn't it?'

Such a convulsion passed across Christabel's face that Don tried to forget his buzzing exhaustion and took her out into the garden for a walk. Harry and Kakia sat together by the fire, which she lit although it was June because she had seen Don shivering.

'What on earth does she have to offer him?' said Harry.

'Safety? At least she's not mercurial.'

'Oh dear. Is that really what he's hoping for from her? It's the last thing.'

He blew his nose and looked at his eyes in a mirror to see if they were bloodshot. 'I'm flaked. When are we going to have lunch? Could we go to bed, do you think? Why is it that beautiful women never seem to have any curiosity?'

'It is because they know they're classical? With classical things the Lord finished the job. Ordinary ugly people know they're deficient and they go on looking for the pieces. Do you know why I think he brings her here? I think he wants you to approve of her.'

'Really?'

'I think so. He was very wounded about us. He hero-worships you and you won.'

'Why should he hero-worship me? I'm not half as clever as he is and I could never achieve his sort of celebrity. That's what he admires, isn't it? Brilliance. Doctoring is for dull old Joes.'

'This is the one thing you can't see about him, isn't it? I suppose the feeling he has about you is what I like about him best. In some ways. Sometimes he's so flash and contrary you wonder what the point is of being fond of him, and then there's this at the root of it which he doesn't even talk about. The Christabel thing is really because of you, I think. It's the only way he can beat you.'

'What do you mean?'

'I think that to Don there may be some kind of romantic status about being married. People like us who are only living together haven't quite made it.'

'I don't really understand that. It sounds too conventional for him.'

'No, nor do I. But I think it's right. Marriage isn't really a convention to him. It's more like medals or exams. If he marries her he'll have got a double first. It might even help him about not trusting women. She's so famous and so beautiful that there's practically no need to face having to make love to her. Jesus, that sounds cold-blooded. You understand what I mean. He finds it so painful. Nothing in it but distress. With Christabel I have a dreadful feeling there'd be a lot of other people who'd be doing it for him anyway.'

'Oh dear.' Harry tapped out his pipe.

'Though he might be in love with her. Do you think that's possible? I didn't allow for that. Dear God, I hope not. That would be the most destructive thing of all.'

The sight of them together offered no deep clue. Christabel looked healthy, receptive and inexhaustible. Don seemed nervous, in a way that Harry and Kakia couldn't understand for the moment. He listened to Christabel's truisms without his usual habit of turning received ideas upside down to make mock-epigrams. Even her effusiveness merely seemed to strike him as a version of the native flamboyance that he most admired. Beside her, painfully, he lost his own colour and became an acolyte. When she beamed her brutal naivete in his direction he seemed to accept it as refreshing and forthright. There was something repulsive about her sincerity, and it made even Harry shrivel into irony in her presence. Her guilelessness was allied with unremitting ambition and it was hard to believe that it ever cost her anything. Like some Victorians, she had a drive that was a peculiar combination of dreaming Utopianism and the most matter-of-fact and slaughterous spite. Her sunny malice had crushed many more melancholy and good-natured actors whom she had worked with. Her unkindness always seemed to be totally idle and not even to involve the effort of temper, which was one of the reasons why it could wear others to the bone. When she was making a film, for instance, she would borrow the engagement ring of a young costume designer as though she were bestowing a favour, or perhaps the fur coat of a small-part young actress, and then lose it on the set or while she was swimming, or simply go on wearing it. At the same time she was always insistent that other people should be good Socialists, though she avoided the word Socialism if she could and called it 'the business of how to live with one another.'

Kakia suggested lunch, but Christabel suddenly cried out and clapped her hands: 'I've cooked you a wholemeal loaf with real stone-ground flour. It's as a present to our weekend, and we must eat it with some lovely fresh cheese and salad in front of the fire.'

Don said wearily that he had eaten two midnight lunches on the plane but would have some coffee. So Kakia put away a steak and kidney pie that she and Harry had been looking forward to ever since six o'clock that morning, and they had Christabel's loaf. Christabel exclaimed about the quality of the watercress and the quality of the lettuce, which was ordinary, and left the loaf to the others because she was watching her diet.

'I'm so tired I can hardly lift my eyelashes,' said Kakia to Harry in the kitchen. 'The mascara weighs a ton.'

'Perhaps we could suggest they'd like to have a sleep.'

Don said that he wanted to have a ride with Harry. Harry looked so beat that Kakia said she would like to go instead. At least she was on Harry's nag, which had a prosperous and forgiving view of the world in spite of a past that seemed much less fortunate than Don's acid horse's. When Don was riding his horse it went perfectly of course. Kakia looked at his tall lean frame and pondered about why it was that whenever she passed a shop window she could see herself to be sitting on her own horse in a way that made its back much longer than usual and its withers higher than its head. Sometimes the progression of its head, neck and back seemed to take as long to pass the window as a naval convoy, and the way she was sitting on the thing was clearly at the root of it, for Don's horse today looked half as long as when she rode it. It was perhaps something to do with the grip of her thighs, or keeping her ankles down, but it certainly wasn't worth the physical effort of doing anything about either. On the gallops Don kept politely reining back and talking to her in the middle of chaos without even seeming breathless. She enjoyed galloping, as long as it was Harry's horse and as long as she could hold on to the saddle, which pinned her crutch into place on the trampoline, but having to talk when the breath was being beaten out of her was simply not possible.

'You haven't asked me about America,' he said perfectly smoothly. She was quite incapable of answering because she had no breath to spare at all.

He went ahead of her down a difficult track, he and the horse picking their way delicately on shiny shale. Harry's horse slipped constantly and often stopped on the bias with no apparent reason or malcontent. Harry had a theory that it had been a milk-pony during the war, and had grown used to choosing its own stops and sliding its hooves across the pavement to wheedle children in basement flats for sugar. The skidding terrified Kakia and she got off and walked. Don looked back eventually and she thought he was probably mocking her, but physical fear was something that he understood. At the bottom of the slope she tried to mount again but every time she put her foot in the stirrup the animal moved and she then dug her toe into its ribs without meaning to, so that it dragged her along some more. She started laughing but she was also very nearly crying because she was overtired, and Don rode back to catch the reins of her horse.

'We might have a drink,' he said. He had filled a whisky flask. They sat under a chestnut tree for a while and Kakia suddenly felt aware of more good nature and conviviality in him than for a long time. He asked her things about Harry and kept saying 'Yes, I see that.' Then he asked her why she wasn't doing any drawing,

'There's the weekly one now.'

'Yes. I know that. But what else?'

'That's enough for me for the minute. It seems to be happening almost too fast as it is. For years I couldn't get plugged into this country. Or perhaps it was the period. I can't tell. And now it's altogether changed and I have a very strong feeling of belonging to the time again. It's like Poland in the war. Now I'm thirty-one and the tracks of my life have been set, I suppose. Anything I do now won't be a change, and I never thought the feeling of being out of key would change either. But people now suddenly seem to understand what I draw. I tried for years to put down the sort of people who were going to cause Suez and from a foreigner it was only resented. Then Suez happened and by that time it was easier.'

'You should go back to Poland. You should have come when, I asked you to before.'

'It wasn't a very practical idea then. I didn't particularly want to get locked up.'

'You wouldn't be after Gomulka.'

'It's simply not very pressing. Perhaps I'll go with Harry one day.'

'I think you're avoiding it because of Andrzej.'

She thought about this. 'It's true that he has an effect.

But the real reason is that I don't belong in Poland any longer, and yet I couldn't draw it without wanting to be involved in it. I don't like possessive exiles. I don't relish the idea of carrying on like some disappointed lover. You can't keep too many nationalities in the air at once. It's like juggling around with a paternity suit and keeping up a fiction about who's the father. In the end it simply doesn't matter very much to anyone at all and no one remembers the truth, not even yourself. Andrzej's done this. He's a professional cosmopolitan and he's cancelled himself out.'

It started to rain, and the warm drops splashed on to the big leaves.

'When I was young I used to carry around a bathplug, of all things, but it was useful if there was any water. I saved it from our house in Poland. In Moscow it got stolen and the last brick seemed to have gone. I didn't belong anywhere for years after that. Now I live here and by some piece of luck I have an instinct for what's happening at the moment. It's a feeling like being properly tuned. When I go out in the streets or to dance halls or football matches, what I see seems sharp and exact and I feel part of it. I've never felt anything like it. When Harry's out on a case at night I draw till my back aches and my knuckles burn because I'm frightened I'll lose it. I never expected it would get any easier, that's the thing. It used to be so much more difficult. I can't get over my good fortune. And Harry as well. I love him with all my heart.'

He looked at her and saw that she was crying, but both of them had done it in front of each other often enough.

'Should you really be going into management on a musical?' she said. 'Is it Christabel's idea?'

'Don't you get very bored by Harry's doctoring, someone like you?' he said, with his usual instant flight into attack. 'Science. Does it really mean anything to anyone but scientists? It must be like being walled up with a morbid garage mechanic. It's such an unadventurous discipline. Politically. Medicine would be a more interesting science if it weren't pegged intellectually to the conservatism of the human body.'

'You do talk a lot of bullshit, don't you? Why a musical? What's it about?'

'A factory that makes nuclear warheads. Christabel wrote it.'

There was a grim pause.

'Half-wrote it,' he went on. 'Someone she knew wrote the other half.'

'Someone she had it off with?'

'You've no right to ask that.'

'Why ever not?' The reason was clear enough in his face; she saw that he could smell pity for himself in the air, like a horse smelling fire.

'All right,' she said. 'As you would say, the only real question is whether it's any good. Ok.'

'I think the music is marvellous. I think it would be thrilling to manage a musical with a big star. The American musical is the only theatrical form with any real popular vitality.'

She resisted rising to this casual jibe and thought a little. 'You should write some more for television, like the programme about 1917,' she said.

'But you hated that.'

'Whoever said so?'

'I always assumed you detested it.'

'But I wrote you a letter about it.'

He shrugged. 'You'd never wanted it to happen. It was an intrusion. You wanted it to be more personal about Jean Boileau. You were being kind to me and making an effort.' He had a remarkable instinct sometimes for the analysis of other people's affectionately-inspired deceits. He calculated always on the assumption that their real responses were as undisclosed as his own, and he was naturally sometimes right.

'It's true,' she said, 'that I kept staring at the set wanting it to produce something that didn't come. I suppose I was hoping that more of Jean would appear out of it. That it would tell me something new about him.'

The horses were steaming like winter coughs. 'That was irrational of me,' she said, going on with difficulty. 'I realise that. I don't think – I don't think the programme gave anyone much idea of what it actually felt like to be one particular soldier in that situation. It was rather generalised and remote. But I realise you weren't trying to do anything biographical. All the same, the quotations from the letters seemed skimped. And I still can't imagine why you didn't use some of the drawings. They were more eloquent than anything.' Long ago she had spent two days forcing herself to give him the material at all, and the programme in the end had practically brushed it aside. First she had laboriously typed out the letters because she thought she wasn't going to be able to bear to deliver the tattered little bits of paper themselves. Then, after another interval and with just as much difficulty, she had seen that he must be given the sketches if he was to do anything worth doing. After the programme her feelings altered again, and became sheer embarrassment at the lack of instinct and art that could allow him to fail to use the drawings. 'But I suppose that wasn't the programme you were interested in doing. It was about why revolutions fail, wasn't it? And you thought that to do that you had to keep to theory. You thought the mutiny was a revolution that failed because it hadn't got a theme. That was it, wasn't it? Though I don't know that it's quite true. I don't know why revolutions have to be successful to be taken seriously. The ones that don't ride to power and change a régime go into a sort of intellectual doghouse and they're thought to have a moral flaw. It might be just a failure of craftiness, or not having the right maniac on the scene, or something else not particularly despicable. A failed mutiny is more likeable than a revolution by decree like Poland in 1945.'

When they came back Don went to bed because he said he wanted to sleep. So did Kakia, but Christabel didn't. Harry was out of the house calming the lecherous peacocks with more grain. All day Don had plainly been aware of the distant screams of sex but had treated it tacitly as their responsibility. Christabel sat in the sitting-room with her legs curled up on the sofa and talked about her musical. Kakia always found plots difficult to listen to and the back of her eyeballs were frying with boredom. Christabel kept looking round and saying 'This is where there's a wonderful number. I wish you had a piano.'

Could she play the piano as well as everything else? Probably.

'Do you play a lot?' asked Kakia, at what seemed to be the end of the plot.

'And then at the beginning of the next scene I find new heart and decide my life with Hank isn't enough and I take over the factory and we march on Washington,' said Christabel.

'With a big finale,' said Kakia, wondering about coffee.

'There's a sub-plot I haven't told you about with a daring part for a Negress.' She started again at the beginning and told her where the sub-plot came in. Kakia got up after that and made some China tea with lemon, which Christabel said she liked better than coffee, and by the time she came back Christabel had picked up a book about African mythology which Kakia had left in front of her with the hope of engaging her attention. She put a cup of tea beside her as quietly as possible, and saw Harry creep crawlingly round the corner from the kitchen and up the stairs to the bedroom. After ten minutes or so she quietly found her car keys and made for the front door because she thought of the village hairdresser as a place where she could sleep under the dryer. Her own bedroom was barred because she didn't want to wake Harry, and dozing in front of Christabel seemed an improbable hope. She got through the door and out of the garage, but Christabel's two-seater was in front of the garage doors and it was too heavy for her to push it more than an inch or two. The curious thing was that, though the car had been standing in the open air for hours, the white leather still reeked of busy-baby. Kakia had her head down to shove when Christabel suddenly appeared and looked amused and said she would love to drive her anywhere she wanted in her beautiful new car, whioh was a remember-me present from darling Don before he went to America.

Kakia said truculently that she was going to the hairdresser. 'The *hairdresser*, darling? On a Sunday?'

'He works at the weekend because of socials at the Mothers' Union. It's only a room really. He shuts on Mondays and Tuesdays instead.'

The explanation sounded so like the lie that Kakia would gladly have told if she had been able to think of a useful one that she felt hard done by, since it happened to be the truth. She let Christabel drive her there in order to demonstrate her blamelessness, and thereby sabotaged herself.

Christobel drove beautifully, fast and heavily, like a German chauffeur, and turned out to have won some particularly famous rallies. Instead of dropping Kakia and coming back for her later, she said benevolently that she would love to come and wait with a magazine. She talked all the time Kakia was being shampooed, charming the surprised hairdresser with compliments about the Italian knack of the way he put in the rollers.

Kakia looked longingly at the dryer where she could perhaps still escape into sleep, as if it were a tub of water and she a man with his clothes on fire. But when she was under it Christabel sat beside her, leaning forward amicably with a cup of Nescafe balanced on her knee, talking loudly through the drone of the dryer and often lifting up the hood of it in case Kakia couldn't hear.

At dinner Christabel remembered that she had seen an old set of children's bows and arrows beside the garage and decided she wanted to play a game outdoors, shooting at the dinner-table candles set into milk-bottles. Don leapt up, seeing something that could perhaps be improvised and salvaged from an evening that he knew very well to be disastrous. Because of his anxiety about Harry's opinion of Christabel he had been taunting Kakia with an invention about Andrzej that had run out of control. He could see that it had troubled Harry, and made Kakia fall silent, but he was quite incapable of stopping. He had watched her and said suddenly that she looked like an old prune tonight, though the thought going through the back of his mind was that her face interested and affected him profoundly and that it always would. She had laughed, though she was in distress, and said that she was more used to him saying that she looked like a desiccated monkey.

Then Don had asked why Kakia had left Sal to look after Harry's baby when Harry was so fond of it.

'Because he's primarily Sal's baby,' said Harry, 'and she's fond of him too, and I'm too busy to do my share of looking after him and it would all fall on Kakia.' He spoke with the firmness that she heard flashing out now and then on the telephone to panicky patients. 'You should have lots of children,' said Don to Harry: 'No I shouldn't' he said; 'I'm far too selfish.'

'I can see you as a Victorian father. Sixteen pretty little girls at the breakfast table,' Harry cut him off and Kakia said suddenly:

'Everyone of us here is an only child.'

She saw then that Harry had thought of this before.

'I'm not,' said Christabel. 'I've got a younger sister.'

It had been then, perhaps because she was remembering games long ago, that Christabel announced her idea about the bows and arrows. It was even possible that she did it to distract the others as best she could from what they had been talking about, for in the garden she suddenly said to Kakia with real kindness.

'You mustn't mind Don.'

'Oh no. But he shouldn't go on at Harry about children.'

Harry was very good at the game. He looked beautiful, said Christabel; his chest expansion was magnificent.

'Is it?' he said modestly. 'Victorian girls used to do archery for the same reason.' His arrow made another ping on a bottle with a candle in it.

'Surgeon's hand,' said Christabel.

Don for once sank his competitiveness and his boredom at games that he turned out not to be good at, and collected the arrows like a ball-boy. After a long time he disappeared to make them all some hot whisky and lemon, for it had grown very cold. Christabel was wearing a sheepskin-lined dufflecoat of

Harry's and her face glowed smoothly in the pale night air. There was a moon, and the candles lit up the bottom branches of an old apple tree. Don looked at Kakia's lined, witty face with love and affection. He knew that his expressions generally misrepresented what he felt, because this was what he had trained them to do, so when she happened to catch him watching her he expected her to look back accusingly in the belief that she was only being mocked again; but apparently his mood was plainer to her than he thought. They sat out of doors then for a long time with the hot tumblers in their hands, lying in deck chairs with rugs over them like four people on a voyage. Then Kakia and Christabel went to bed and Don helped Harry to put away the chairs.

'You and Kakia should have children,' he said again, wanting to recover what he had said by giving it a different inflection. Harry said nothing, but later smiled at him warmly out of no immediate context and asked about the musical.

'Christabel's very beautiful,' he said.

'I'm longing to work with her,' said Don. 'She's totally professional. She works everyone to a standstill.'

'That sounds oppressive. Is it?'

'Hard work is life. You know how I hate holidays.

'But we had a good time in Turkey, didn't we? I did.'

'That was different. I've never enjoyed one like that.'

Most holidays are like New Year's Eve, or office parties. Full of fleeting disappointments and silly projects about getting brown or making the switchboard girl.'

'You always make me feel unpurposeful. I suppose I'm irredeemably lazy. My life is really one long passion for the typing pool. I do love girls, their clothes, and the way they cope. I really worship them. They're quite different from us. Quite, quite different. They try to make things work. If life could be a holiday always, waking up and going to sleep at the wrong time –' He grinned. 'I'm sure that's the real practical, disreputable reason why I don't mind night call you know. I really quite like them. They break up the pattern.' They had another drink. 'You're not being used by Christabel, are you? said Harry.

'I don't know if I am or not.' Harry was the only person in the world to whom Don would ever say such a thing. 'If I am, I can't help it.' They left it.

'Kakia looked tired,' said Don.

'We were up all night with your bloody peacocks.'

'They have to be shut up when they're mating.'

'I thought I remembered that was what you used to do, but I couldn't think where you put them.'

'I'll do it tomorrow.'

'Kakia is more than an only child. She was the child of the only time her parents even shared the same bedroom. I'd wanted you to know that at dinner. Her uncle told her about it just as she was supposed to be leaving for England at the beginning of the War. His sister had told him once and he remembered it. The uncle was a dentist and I suppose he was used as a confessor. The one-shot child. Mum sounds a dilly. It seems a harsh little story to have exiled a thirteen-year-old with, but I suppose it's the sort of thing you do when you're afraid you may not see someone again.'

'She's very happy. You know that, don't you? I saw Sal in New York,'

'Was she all right?'

'Lots of parties. Very popular. She asked a lot of questions. I was glad I hadn't seen you lately.'

Kakia was asleep when Harry went up. He watched her from the window-seat for a long time hoping she might wake, missing her acutely, but she was deeply unconscious. When he went to sleep himself he remained aware of her breathing and a change in it woke him. He put a hand on her to break a dream and she started and shivered like a dog. Hours later he woke again and this time she was awake herself, and they played a game they had made up called logosthenics.

'What's a widget?' she said to him.

'A widget,' he said, inventing cheerfully with a look daring her to better it, 'is a late fifteenth-century instrument used to separate the warp from the woof in tapestry.'

'No it isn't. It's the device you use to let some air into the top of a game bag. The dead birds have to have oxygen as soon as they're dead or else the taste is spoilt.'

'Do you know anything about game bags?'

'I don't even know anything about game. I can't think of any words. Your turn.'

'I've dried up. Sometimes one can't think of anything except real words. I just thought of tommyrot,' said Harry.

'That's a good one.'

'I know, but it's a real word. Like the time you thought you'd made up mollycoddle.'

'I've got one. What's a mimmybrace?'

'Ah, that's a very interesting word,' he said heavily.

'You're stalling.'

'No I'm not.

It's a small loop made of tapestry and leather –'

'You've got stuck on things about tapestry. This isn't going to be any good.'

'Oh yes it is. As I say, it's the small loop of tapestry and leather that was used in the eighteenth century to hold back a woman's skirt on a side saddle.'

'That's not at all bad. But I'll tell you what it really is. You know the little boys of nine and ten who were pressed into the Navy to be midshipmen in whatever century it was? When they were sent into the crow's nest to keep a lookout they were often so tired that they fell asleep on the watch, so the second officer used to put a mimmybrace inside their jacket, which was a long narrow board studded with nails to keep them awake.'

'My God, that's very believable. Oh yes, I believe that. Poor little beasts!' He lay on one side and pulled his knees up.

'Did that make your balls hurt?'

'Yes.'

'Try another one.'

He tried to think. 'What's guidenhorn?' he said.

'Guidenhorn. I can't do that one. You've decided, haven't you? What is it?'

'Guidenhorn,' he said in a Scottish Voice, is the Highland name for the feast of a bride's maidenhead. The Maconochie is richt merry tonight and the sundering of guidenhorn can be heard from Skye to Carlisle.'

'I think that's as nasty as the mimmybrace.' She got up and looked out of the window. 'Would you like some Bovril?'

'Not much. I'd rather have a brandy.'

'I don't know why I like Bovril, I think it reminds me of liver extract.'

She came back with a mug of Bovril and a big brandy.

'What's withen?' she said. He had nearly gone to sleep while she was away.

'I haven't the faintest idea, but you're obviously longing to tell me. I was asleep.'

'No you weren't, you were half asleep. You are just trying to pass the time until you got the brandy.

'Get on with it. What's withen?'

'Withen is a term in merchant banking.'

'That's a good idea.'

'Withen is the half-hour in the week when the Bank of England is closed but merchant banking goes on. The Bank of England closes half past twelve on a Saturday, you see, but the adding up or whatever they do, the buying of shares, goes on till one. In that half-hour you're not in credit, you're in withen.' They drank and listened to the bush baby waking up in the bathroom.

'What time have we got to leave?'

'Quarter to eight.'

'We've still got three hours.

Is that allowing for the traffic?'

'I've got someone on till ten. God, there are the peacocks. Even Don can't keep them quiet.' He thought for a moment, and then said 'Good.' After another silence, when she thought he had gone to sleep, he said: 'I wish we had the life of those bleeding birds. Nothing but lust all day.'

'What's lust? Let's try it with real words.'

'I can't do lust,' he said after a time. 'It sounds a bit like a bath cleaner to keep S-bends sparkling but I'm not altogether happy about it.'

'Yes, I know. If you don't invent at once it's no good! All right then. What's arse? Quick.'

'Arse is an ancient language that the folksong society is trying to revive,' he said immediately.

She thought about this with pleasure and they went to sleep. At half past seven, when he was eating a piece of Christabel's loaf and black cherry jam in his fingers, moving softly so as not to wake them upstairs, he put his arms round her and said: 'I don't know anyone else I could play that with. My brain ticks over too slowly with other people, I can never get over my good fortune.'

'Yes,' she said.

IX

'But she's not in pain?' said Harry on the telephone to a patient's husband.

'She might be in pain but not feeling it.'

'Is she frightened?'

'I just think she'd be happier if you came round, doctor.'

Harry put the receiver down and got out of bed. It was 4.30 in the morning three years later. He and Kakia were still living in her Broad Court attic.

'I'd better go.'

'Who is it?'

'Mrs Lomas. He was ringing from a callbox. I don't know why he didn't use the one at home. He didn't make any sense, but still.'

'What did he say?'

'She seems all right. I expect she's in a panic. She was frightened last time I saw her and I suppose it still seems a long time to go. Two more months.'

'I hate night calls like this. Often they don't seem quite candid. Don't go. She's not miscarrying, is she? You're exhausted.'

'He said she might be in pain but not feeling it.' She shook her head at him. 'I know, but there was some sort of signal he was trying to make. People say the wrong things in the night.'

The Lomases lived in an airless house in Lisson Grove. Harry had the impression that Mr Lomas was a rather stupid man and that his wife, who was much cleverer than he was, had lost the gift of forbearance with him since she was pregnant and started to humiliate him. He had always seen them before in his clinic and the poor, brassy house surprised him; her air had implied more. He started to go upstairs. Mr Lomas, who was fully dressed, pulled him back roughly towards a door and said:

'It's in there.'

What was 'it'? Anxiety? Trouble? An animal?

A girl who wasn't Mrs Lomas was sitting fiercely on the sofa. Her cheeks were burning and she was either feverish or in a temper.

'He dragged me here. I didn't want to come. There's nothing wrong with me,' she said.

'She's not well,' said Mr Lomas, giggling. Harry turned round quickly, but it was true; he was giggling.

Harry took her temperature and looked at her throat and told her that she might have mild tonsillitis.

'There's nothing wrong with me,' she said again snappily.

'Who's your doctor?' he said. She told him. He looked at Mr Lomas. 'What are you thinking of, calling me out like this in the middle of the night for someone who isn't my patient and isn't even in pain?'

'Well, doc, she looked to me as if she had a temperature. I didn't actually say who it was for, did I? I thought if I said the wrong name you wouldn't come.' Again the man giggled and slapped Harry on the back. Everything seemed jocular; nothing was serious. Mr Lomas offered Harry a drink from a trolley made of mirror and white wrought iron. It was the only thing in the room that wasn't shabby.

Harry said no, but sat down on the dingy sofa.

'He had a dust-up with her about me, if you want to know,' said the girl.

'Six months ago,' said Mr Lomas. 'She couldn't care less now.'

'I don't want to know at all,' said Harry. 'Is Mrs Lomas asleep?'

'Nothing to worry about,' said Mr Lomas.

'What she said to him was that he didn't have no intention of getting anywhere and he'd always be at the bottom of the heap. That was what got me,' said the girl.

Harry went upstairs without asking and found the bedroom. Mrs Lomas was asleep. She was snoring as pregnant women often do, and in the dark her face seemed to Harry to have changed shape. She suddenly started awake and switched on the light and he saw that she had a handkerchief stuffed into her mouth. She sat up without surprise and said:

'I suppose he got you here for her. Is she still here?'

'He said he didn't think you were well.'

'There's nothing wrong with me. I haven't been crying, if that's what you think. He says I snore and I stuff my mouth up to try to breathe through my nose. I hate sounding like this.' She looked close enough to weeping.

'I don't suppose the sleeping pills help,' he said. 'I'll give you something else.' He hesitated, and then said: 'Who is she?'

'She's quite a nice girl really. They were having an affair but I didn't give tuppence. I was glad in a way. It left me alone. He's bored with her now. It's over. She doesn't see any future in him. He was driving me crackers. Silly man, he left clues all over the place. It was the stupidity more than anything.'

'What's he got her here for in the middle of the night, then?'

'He can do what he likes. He said he was lonely. I don't know. It's to show her off, I expect. It's what he wants, isn't it?' She was covering up, for he could see now clearly enough that she had been crying, but if she needed a pretence he thought it better to leave her with it. Her side of the bed was piled with books and papers; if she could read she must be fairly all right.

'He called me out for you, you know. She's got mild tonsillitis, I think, but it was your name he used.'

'That was to get you here.'

'Yes, that's true. But it was also because he was worried about you. He felt responsible for both of you. I expect he felt guilty. I'll try to get her away, shall I?'

She shrugged and then smiled. 'If you can. He'll think I wouldn't know either way. He sleeps in the other room now because he says I keep him awake. He thinks I'm such a fool. I hear everything he does.' Then the tears began to flow. 'We haven't earned any money since you made me stop working. He doesn't make a bean. He spends it all.'

'You might have lost the baby. I'm sorry. You should have told me. Perhaps we can do something.'

'I know he's spending it all on her. I know it.'

'Come on. An evening at the Ace of Spades once a month. Probably not even that.'

'It's always been my money we've lived on. I bought it all. This house. He pays the rates and that's it. You don't know how it feels. Stuck here and not earning anything. We haven't got anything left. I had to write to my sister for a loan and I can't bring myself to post it.' She fumbled on the side table but the letter was buried somewhere. When she unlocked a drawer Harry saw neat piles of half crowns and two-shilling pieces and a traveller's cheque book. She flushed and didn't explain them.

'He never thinks. I know he's going to get into terrible trouble one day. I go on at him for having half a brain but it's no good, is it? I bully him and try to sharpen him and he only gets duller. Do you think he needs some drugs? Sometimes I wonder if there's something missing in his diet. He doesn't seem to make connections. He contradicts himself and doesn't see it. He even incriminates himself and doesn't notice. I can feel that I frighten him by thinking faster than he does and going on at him, and that makes him worse. I sit and sit up here reading to keep out of his way and he seems all right and then I can feel myself pouncing on him for something quite trivial.'

Harry was quite sure now that the telephone call genuinely had been for the wife's sake, because of some scene that had run out of Mr Lomas's control, and that the giggles downstairs were made of insufficiency and remorse.

'You're being soft with yourself,' he said sharply. 'Pregnancy often makes people feel melodramatic. It's because you've got something to face that you're suddenly frightened of because you can't get out of it. I don't blame you. I'd be edgy. Probably I'd behave worse. But don't pretend it's anything else. Don't blame it on the wrong thing.'

'You try it.'

'You've got enough money really, haven't you?'

'No. Well, just. It's all *going*. As long as I get back to work quickly.'

When he went downstairs the girl had her coat on and the man was still laughing in a high voice.

'Afraid it was a wild goose chase, doc,' he said.

'She's a bit frightened, isn't she?' said Harry. He decided to speak in front of the girl. 'She's bothered about not earning at the moment. You might see if you can think of a way to be reassuring. Both of you.'

The girl muttered. 'Grinding his face in the mud for losing his job. It wasn't his fault.'

'She didn't tell me you were out of a job.'

Mr Lomas stopped laughing. 'Didn't she?'

'Nothing.'

Mr Lomas's voice had quite changed. 'Well, I didn't expect that. Did you, Mavis? That was good of her, wasn't it?'

'I suppose so.'

'There,' said Mr Lomas triumphantly to Harry. 'We've got a good marriage, you see. It's a good home, no doubt about it. How many wives, eh? She trusts me, you see. Doesn't she? Even Mavis sees it.'

'She'll trust you when you get a job, that's the thick and the thin of it. Hanging about the house with a face like a kipper.'

'I'll get one in no time now. No need to worry about that. You won't see Lomas for dust. I tell you, doc, you need a drink, turning out at this hour.'

Harry accepted the *crème de menthe* that was given to him. As he went to the door Mr Lomas tried to put some pound notes into his hand. 'Cash', he said. 'Diddle the tax-man, eh?'

'It's on the health service,' said Harry crisply. He felt he had taken too long to perceive the real trouble, and that when he had seen it he had still dealt with it inadequately. Relatives on night calls were often as disturbing as patients: they were captious and explosive, with veins of tyranny and deceit. But by the morning he saw it differently himself and thought that the Lomases might well be better off with each other today than for some time. When Mrs Lomas came to see him a week later she volunteered that he had got a new job and sounded quite protective about him.

X

Harry: I dreamt I was ill in hospital, not very badly, and Don and Christabel were there and suddenly I couldn't see her. I could make out Don but not her. You told me she was there and you described her in a low voice and held my hand. I think I was blind.

Kakia: I dreamt my mouth was stopped up and I couldn't speak to you. I drew for you but the ink faded as soon as I drew. You kept the pieces of paper in your wallet all the same. I couldn't eat and I got thin and hideous. It was like the war. A man was sick in the street when he saw me.

Harry: I dreamt we had a holiday in Trafalgar Square, Just the two of us. We took a month off and it rained the whole time. We sent postcards saying how rotten the weather was and had the best time of our lives.

Kakia: I dreamt we had a baby and I was giving her a bottle one day when she was five or six weeks old and she suddenly pushed the bottle on one side and said she didn't like milk. Only she spoke in Polish. I couldn't get her to learn English.

Harry: I dreamt the most boring dream I've ever had in my life. It was all talk, at a dinner party where nobody was quite serious but everyone spoke tragically. It was like being in some awful art film about alienation. I bored myself so much that tears came into my eyes and I woke up flaked.

Kakia: I dreamt that you were Jean and I was my mother, and you were going away in uniform on a train and I'd forgotten to give you your gas mask. I ran and ran after you with it and a glass bubble grew in the back of my throat and reached out of my mouth so that I couldn't breathe. They shot you because you hadn't got the gas mask and my father found me and wouldn't let me look for your body.

Kakia: I dreamt I was an old woman in a concentration camp and a little girl ran after me shouting 'Mother' and I said 'She's nothing to do with me.'

They had these dreams, and many others, which became part of their lives, as dreams will. When they could remember them they generally told them to each other. Harry's usually came back to him after an interval, during one of the fits of talkativeness that fell on him when he was looking for something after breakfast. Kakia's were lucid for a few minutes and then gone; she often clung onto his shoulder the moment she woke up and talked to him with a pressure so like the push of a bore that it made him laugh. They both longed urgently for a child, but forbore from speaking much about it to each other because nothing must be spoilt. Harry was shy for her privacy, afraid that his job might abuse the meaning of children for her; Kakia dreamt of her barren carcase over and over again as a faulty machine, until one day the image of herself as a dud gadget became so ridiculous that she woke up laughing. 'Not another dream,' he said sleepily. She went on laughing and decided not to tell him, and that particular nightmare stopped.

'Shouldn't we have Dr Shitbag back to dinner?' she said.

'You didn't like him. Last time you called him Fartface.'

'Yes. But perhaps it was just a bad evening. I feel as if I should try. You're always doing things for me.'

'He's not too bad. As long as you don't leave us alone like last time.'

'That wasn't my fault. She took me up to her bedroom and wouldn't stop. I shouldn't think he ever opens his mouth to her. She went on and on about public schools. They're sending their son somewhere or other and she says they'd have sent him to the local place except that you can't make a gesture with somebody else's life. I don't know why it's less of a gesture to send him to Charterhouse than round the corner.'

Harry hesitated. 'If you really mean you can stick it. But if there's going to be a fight it would be better not to do it at all.'

'Perhaps we could have them with Ambrose and Don on Thursday. That would make it easy.'

'Will Christabel be coming?'

'Will she be back from New York?'

'Tuesday.'

'Then I suppose he's meaning to bring her. I wish he didn't always say "I" when he means "we". I see the point about not behaving like some two-piano act but it would be nice to know. What about Ambrose?'

Harry laughed and said that the sight of Ambrose and Christabel locking horns might not be a bad way of satisfying old Shitbag. 'If we can give him something to gripe at it'll be easy,' he said. 'Whenever I see him I do my best but we don't seem to grumble at the same things. Last time we were coming away from a patient he went out of his mind about people in new towns. He said they want the Health Service to get better and better every year, like washing machines. When he put it like that I had to say that I thought perhaps I did too.'

Ambrose suspected Christabel of unkindness to Don, but he also suspected Don of being queer without admitting it to himself, his attitude to her was not much more than enormously and incredulously watchful. His eyes literally enlarged in her presence and sometimes seemed to have stopped blinking. It was clear to everyone but her that he was egging her on, but she was never aware of being a phenomenon to him. He had said a few months ago that she was the 1960 drophead model of Miss Boddenham the magazine editor whom he still worked with, and that she could turn a political anxiety into an item of needlework the moment she opened her mouth. Her declarations about public affairs would have been well liked if they had merely been sentimental; what made them hard to forgive was their talent for inspiring guilt and cynicism in people whose capacity for enthusiasm she had managed to sour and who would otherwise have enjoyed feeling simple themselves.

The doctor sat beside Kakia at dinner and asked whether there was garlic in the soup.

'No,' she said, 'only onion. Harry'd rather keep off garlic except at weekends because of breathing it over patients. I thought you would too.'

'Can't stand the stuff,' he said. 'There's a new pizza place where we live and the smell's like a dago army camp. Muriel went there once and I wouldn't let her near me for two days.'

'I'm sorry, dear,' said his wife. 'I thought it might be somewhere different for us to go. If you wanted.'

'You have lots of garlic where you come from, I suppose,' he said to Kakia, pushing his soup away rudely and buttering his bread.

'Not particularly.'

'I thought it was all garlic; garlic and *The Bartered Bride* in Czechoslovakia.'

'Isn't it Poland?' said his wife.

'Oh, sorry. Hope I haven't dropped a brick. Doctors aren't up to much on politics, you know. Too busy seeing the meat, I'm afraid.' His laugh was loud and unpleasant; there was something about it that led one to feel that his emotional life must be primitive.

'I read the other day that no Russian peasant will kick a man who's standing up,' said his wife. 'You may knock him down and then kick him, but you have to wait till he's lying down. Isn't that interesting? Exactly the opposite way round to us.'

'Very wise,' said Ambrose.

'Dead true,' said Kakia.

Christabel put down her knife and fork and looked at them both severely. 'I don't think that's funny,' she said. 'It's no use indulging our feelings of nationalism. We've got to live with the Russians. I know you've gone through a lot, Kakia, but sometimes I think you can't see the wood for the trees. Russia does at least try to conduct its life so as to make the good things available to everyone.'

'Russians have always been hugely concerned with ethics and hardly at all with conduct,' said Don.

She turned the beam of her face on to him and it was like the forgiveness of sins. 'I know you don't mean that.'

'Don't go on,' he said, shaking his head.

'People often get embarrassed about anyone in the arts having political views. But it's part of *life*, isn't it? My mere existence is a political act. I can't help it.'

'I daresay Kakia feels that too,' said Don.

'Do you know who first said "Discussion with rifles"?' said Kakia.

'Stalin,' said Don.

'No, Lenin in 1922.'

'What do you mean by that, sweetheart?' said Christabel.

'I suppose I only mean that it was there right from the start. Rosa Luxembourg saw what was happening and got assassinated for it. If you repress speech and books and newspapers and meetings and try to run a socialist country through closed circles of dogmatists who won't take expert advice or meet people or open themselves up to any experience at all, then how can life possibly be anything but brutalised?'

'I agree with you,' said Christabel, 'that if one were in the arts – and even then only the creative arts, not the performing arts – or in politics, of course, you'd be worse off in a Communist country. But not if you were in industry. Or science.' Her voice sounded flirtatious but combative, perhaps to rile Don. Kakia said nothing. But Christabel pushed her and said 'What's your answer to that?'

'It would depend what sort of scientist. Since Stalin boobed about the bomb and didn't believe in it because it wasn't dogmatically feasible, some things are easier. You'd be allowed to read foreign journals, for instance. Sometimes you'd even be allowed to be wrong. If you were a physiologist you'd be well off. If you were a geneticist or a plant biologist you'd probably long since have had Lysenko's little hatchet up your jumper. If you were Einstein you'd have been generously rehabilitated by *Pravda*, which stopped calling you an idealistic babbler five whole years ago. Words can have upside down meanings, you see. One gets used to it in time. Idealistic can be a very rude word when it's used officially. Democrat is rude when it's used unofficially. A democrat in spoken Polish is understood to mean a privileged bastard. A demo-crate is a big car used by a Party official to drive around in the rubble.'

'You're railing about 1949, sweetheart,' said Christabel. 'It's all changed.'

'The only real kind of change is one that can't be reversed by decree. How many of those have there been? Not many in Poland. Not as much as they thought in 1956, not what they dearly hoped for, not nearly. In England, perhaps, quite a lot.'

'Your Central European bitterness doesn't depress me,' said Christabel. 'Sometimes I wonder where the Poles got their reputation for heroism.'

'Hey,' said Harry angrily.

'Heroism is something that even Catholic Poles have had to learn to outgrow,' said Kakia. 'Do you think it seems heroic to

124

any of us to have had nothing but cavalry in September 1939 against tanks that came through our frontiers in streams fifteen kilometres wide, in weather that was supposed to bog the tanks in mud but went on dry and burning day after day? On September 2 in the afternoon there was a wind, and we hoped, but the rain never came. There's no such thing as a heroic country any longer. Heroism for a nation murders too many people. There are only people who are more or less honourable. The most that any of us can hope to be is a little less weak than usual.'

'I suppose that's the famous Polish irony,' said Christabel, looking as if she were swatting an insect. Kakia shook her head, unable to speak. 'I call it defeatism. I must say it sounds all too like the voice of England too. The only place in England where I get a real feeling of hope is in a pub.'

'*What* pub?' said Ambrose.

'We don't go to pubs much, do we, dear?' said the doctor's wife mournfully.

'I mean the atmosphere. Cheerfulness and honesty and wonderful, wonderful effort and heart. I can feel England there. I think I really am rather a peasant. Whereas Kakia's a typical blackhearted bourgeois,' said Christabel.

'Perhaps that's why you like America so much,' said Ambrose, inflaming Christabel to the top of his bent. 'You think America's a peasant country, don't you? Like Russia. In Russia they have placards on the wall saying "Have you increased someone's output today?" In America they say "Have you had a nigger to dinner?"'

'*No* one would say that, Ambrose. Having a Negro to dinner is a liberal thing to do and no liberal would say nigger.'

'Christabel,' said Harry. 'You're being sent up.'

'I don't think the efforts of good American liberals are funny.' She turned on Don, still smiling. 'It's all very well for you to sit there saying nothing. It's what I'd expect. I can't bear fence-sitting. We have to *declare.*' She pounded the table, and then smiled still more firmly because she suddenly realised she had brought some sort of curtain down. 'We have to do *this* to life.' She spread her arms widely. Now she was taking her curtain-call and accepting the bouquets. The doctor's wife looked rapt. Christabel was an example beyond emulation: not to her Leonard's taste and impractical in a house with children, but all the same magnificent.

Harry talked to the doctor's wife but found her attention impossible to hold because she kept looking round at Christabel. Don smoked incessantly and put on dark glasses half-way through the meal. Kakia talked quietly to the doctor about medicine while they ate salad and cheese. It was much like an interval in a famous singer's dressing room. Christabel sat silent, refused anything more to eat, smiled steadily, and for several minutes lay her head on the back of her chair with her eyes closed. Then suddenly, as if the next act had started and as though she hadn't been able to hear Kakia talking to the doctor about his job for the last ten minutes, she turned to him with the full candle power of her smile and said:

'Tell us all about the National Health Service.'

'Ah,' he said. 'You must ask our host that one. I'm only the humble GP.'

'I've heard him. I want to know what you think of it.'

'I'm too busy to have an opinion, dear lady! We leave that to the upper echelons.'

'But you're the heart of it, aren't you?'

'The research boys don't think so. We used to be, but not any longer. We're just the fools who do the work now. I call us the prescription-writing boot-boys.'

'One day they'll realise,' recited his wife loyally. 'The best of British medicine is the bedside manner, not the British Research Council. Leonard's got a wonderful bedside manner.'

'I'm *sure*,' said Christabel.

'Isn't it possible for a country to be good at research as well as welfare?' said Ambrose.

'We would all do research if we had *time.* Like our clever friend here. In the old days I used to have time myself. And you know what takes it up now? Not the journals I'd like to read. They pile up and I throw them away in the wrappers. What takes the time is the endless, tiring, *unwarranted* explanations that people expect now. And whose fault is that? The Health Service. Your sponger and your moaner can just walk into your surgery now and pin you there. They've got it on a plate. I was called out once to prescribe a free wig. I ask you. Free cottonwool. Happens all the time.'

'But we always did that anyway, didn't we?' said Harry. 'Before the war, doctors in industrial areas were always handing out free vaseline to rub into men's boots.'

'We've got a public of wets. That's what I call the patients now, a public. We're entertainers now, we're not physicians. England wasn't built by old-age pensioners and molly-coddled no-goods living off the State. Mind you, I have nothing against the pensioners. But half the time theres nothing wrong with them. They've just come in for a talk. Well have I got time? Much as I'd like to.' He pushed his plate away and got out a comb and methodically twanged together two teeth at a time all the way down it, which was a habit he had. 'Many an argument our host and I have had about our famous Welfare State. He's entitled to his opinions but if I may say so he doesn't see the underbelly. I was a do-gooder once myself. But you have to take what you find now. Once I could send a patient packing if I didn't like the look of him. What do I have to do now? See him that's what. What use to me now is this nose I've got for the waster and the malingerer? If I smoke him out, he'll go blubbering off to some patients' grumbling society. You can't get the partners now either. They're all Pakistanis. When I'm interviewing a partner I have him to a meal to see how he eats. I'm no snob, a doctor can't afford to be, but he's going to share your life, isn't he? You can't have the wrong man. Half of them don't even know how to hold a knife.' He looked sharply at his wife. 'They hold it like she does, see what I mean? Not under her palm but between her thumb and finger like a pen. I ask you.'

She had flushed, and put her knife and fork together.

'I don't believe in being hypocritical about the question of having Indians or Catholics in your practice,' he said. 'Some people would say they won't have them because the patients wouldn't like it. I won't have them because I wouldn't like it. What do you think a pregnant woman feels like if she suddenly sees a doctor bending over her whirling a crucifix like a drum major? No thank you very much. And take my advice. Don't get run over on the M1 north of Luton.'

'Why, Leonard?' prompted his wife forgivingly, giving him the cue he wanted.

'Because you'll get an Indian casualty officer, that's why. He'll go over you with a toothcomb and miss the lot. He's got a genius for concentrating on the wrong thing, your Indian. Go to him with a carcinoma and you'll get your in-growing toenail put right.'

'Surely you're being prejudiced,' said Christabel faintly, displaced. 'Tell them about Dr Thing, dear,' said his wife.

'Didn't you read about that? Some wretch called Ram Jam Something-or-other, not that they aren't all, admitted a seventy-eight-year-old emergency who'd fallen downstairs. He had skull X-rays done and there wasn't anything and he sent him home. Two days later the poor sod died and post-mortem showed seven broken ribs, a fractured sternum and a fractured pelvis.'

Kakia wondered whether Harry wanted her to try to do anything, but he was looking at his plate. He would like her perhaps to make things work, to be accommodating; at any rate not to have a fight or take this man to embody medicine. Don and Ambrose, Harry's friends, were both alert and stiff like guard-dogs. Don had taken off his dark glasses to watch him. Ambrose's caustic profile seemed beautiful and bitten away by acid. Harry's face was bent downwards: he had pushed his chair back and was sitting a little sideways against the arm, with his head stooping forward. Kakia could have drawn it that moment in nothing but triangles: cheekbones, chin, eyebrows raised against attack, a triangular bone over his eyes white under the light.

'We could have coffee,' she said. But to make it she would have to leave him.

'I've always wanted to be a doctor,' said the deaf one, stretching. 'It's a vocation. They're right about that. But I've come to the strange decision now that I must look after myself. If a quarter of my patients are pests, nothing wrong with them apart from wanting a word with the priest, i.e. me, that's a quarter of my time and income gone, a quarter of my petrol, a quarter of my secretary's salary, a quarter of my rent, a quarter of my stationery, and a hell of a lot more than a quarter of my telephone bill, considering the attention they demand. Not forgetting wear and tear on instruments. Then there are the stamps. You should see the stamp bill. Well, I've got to be practical about it. Nobody else looks after a doctor. There are some patients I'd never take, just a matter of sizing up temperament. I can smell trouble with them like I can smell an epileptic. With your genuine case I take the most trouble in the medical directory. I'm round there with the milk. I set myself a task, all new temperatures taken by eight thirty. It sounds impossible, doesn't it, but if I don't manage it I disappoint myself. I'd have made a good nursing sister, I'll say that. You have to have a nose for it, as I say, to be able to tell a real one from the kind of bitch who's just on heat for sympathy. You know why I like doctoring? I'll tell you. In the end your tricky ones come home to roost. There's a woman of mine who was the biggest nuisance on my list for twenty years. Now she's got arthritis so she can't move and she's stopped yelling at me and wants to hear my voice for once. That's what they call the reward of time. She really wants to hear me talk now. There's nothing I can do for her but I go, I go. When they say it's a vocation they're not far off it.'

Kakia took Harry away and said that he was ill.

XI

Three months later Harry was prosecuted for aborting an unmarried girl without psychiatric sanction. He was struck off the Medical Register and sent to gaol. The supplanted forces of English reaction found in him their perfect victim: not only could they punish him, they could also exact revenge for an act that had happened to be itself one of the most punishing things he could have asked himself to do. Kakia had known nothing about it, but there was no need to question him about the cost of agreeing to do it.

'Don't waste the time I'm away. Do something with it,' he said. 'They're bound to convict but it shouldn't be long. Only a few months, as we're always trying not to say to one another. I can manage this sort of thing better than you think. It can't be as bad as prep school. I think perhaps I may have the religious temperament after all the spite of not being religious.'

He looked ill, and in the mornings before he was committed he was regularly sick. Yet there was something buoyant about him.

Kakia did what she could to turn the suffering to use. His patients attacked for him and formed a society. There were letters and meetings. People said that at least the case might get reform moving. Ambrose, a Catholic, wrote an exceptionally generous letter to *The Times* about the fiction of the two-signature rule. He finished with an acerbic sentence about the Hippocratic oath and its obligation upon doctors to respect their colleagues and safeguard their patients; he had not realised before, he said, that the order represented a deliberate priority, but there was no doubt now that Dr Clopton should have saved the face of the Royal College of Obstetricians and Gynaecologists before the future of a patient.

For the first few days Ambrose had her to stay with him, but she found it even more impossible to work away from Harry's home than in it. When she went back she found a note from him stuck in the stale butter in the refrigerator. He must have left it there before he went. It said: 'Don't get glum. Remember you're British.'

Don and Christabel were away on holiday in Albania. On the day Harry went to gaol she had a postcard from Don that sounded as if it might have been written when he was drunk. The claims of being wildly happy and of planning to cancel everything and stay for months seemed foolish and unreal; but then so did the tinted wild flowers on the other side. She sent a cable to the likeliest hotel but had no reply. Her instinct that she must tell him what had happened became more urgent every day. At his hotel in London they had had a card saying he was to be in Nice on the 27th of the month. The postmark on it was later than hers so she believed it and went.

He had arrived in Paris the day before but gone out. The concierge said he was travelling alone, and gave her the key with knowing boredom. She went up to his bedroom to wait for him but felt an interloper and came down again. The room looked uninhabited; there were no books out, and the bed clearly hadn't been slept in, for though the room hadn't been cleaned yet the bedspread was on the bed. There was a bottle of marc brandy nearly empty on the dressing table, and damp warmth was still coming from the shower. His clothes were in heaps all over the room; Harry always left his so neatly that she resented them.

She waited downstairs in an old-fashioned writing-room behind the stair well, separated from the concierge's desk by a mahogany telephone box. As the hours went by she learnt the room backwards and thought of describing it to Harry. There was a walnut escritoire in the room, and in it some pretty blue hotel stationery engraved in black with a drawing of the Promenade des Anglais. It was evocative, and he might like it. She wrote the letter to him that was permitted each week, realising even before she started it that she was unlikely to think it was the best one to send, but it was something to do and seemed a way of making contact with him. Writing to a man in prison was like going to see the bedridden: it was wicked to do it in a mood of urgency, because urgency was the very thing they themselves were deprived of. She put the piece of writing paper into her pocket, and asked the concierge how late she could leave the cancellation of her plane booking that evening.

She sat on a chaise-longue that faced the entrance fifty feet away. She tried to read the papers. A maid brought her coffee three or four times and slowly unbent; when the first tray was finished she was about to move Kakia away, but after a while she grew friendly. It was long past dark when Don came back. He was almost running, and he had the sun-glasses on again, even though they made him stumble on the fringe of the carpet. Yet when he took them off to see what had made him trip there was nothing he could have wanted to hide, for he hadn't been crying. It was strange: he looked at the carpet before he said anything to her.

'Whatever are you doing here?' He spoke hoarsely, like someone caught reading pornography.

She tried to get him to attend, but he kissed her and said something meaninglessly effusive.

'Wait,' he said then, 'I've got to telephone.'

He ran upstairs two steps at a time. A few minutes later he raced down again and she heard him shouting at the desk in a French that refused to express him, saying that his telephone was *détruit, kaput, en panne*. The concierge declined for a long time to understand him at all and then told him with vicious speed to use the instrument in the hall. Don went into the callbox and waited for his number, hanging out of the door at an angle like a child standing on a swing and pelting the life out of it. In the end she went to help him; he was trying to get Christabel at another hotel. When he had found her Kakia started to leave, but he grabbed her wrist, and then leant his forehead on the back of his hand with his elbow on the telephone directories. What Christabel was saying was unintelligible, but the things that Don said made it easy enough to fill it in.

'You told me you'd be there.'

'You don't seriously expect me to go to a museum. Do you think I can think about anything –'

'I don't believe he's your son. You're lying . . .'

'Yes I have. I can go to his professors and find out what the real one looks like. If he isn't a fiction too, that is. Which I begin to doubt.'

'You say that and you won't turn up again. I waited there last time for four hours.'

'I know perfectly well who it is. It's that international tart you picked up. I could tell from the way you talked about him. You're mad.'

'I don't want his compliments. I wouldn't have him in any musical, ever –'

'I'm not.'

'I'm *not*. If you'd only tell me. I thought you were always going to tell me.'

Christabel made a kissing noise into the phone and put the receiver down. Don leant his head farther onto his hands.

'She spent four days with me in Albania because she said the flowers were beautiful there and she wanted to go somewhere where there weren't any cars. She let me take her all the way to a place we haven't even got diplomatic relations with, so you can't even complain if you're stuck there. To *look at flowers* and to *walk*. I hate flowers. And we had to go under some official auspices of hers and look at *factories* and *dairy projects*. We were going to be alone and not think about anyone else all summer, and all the time she had a booking in her bag eight days later to go back to the Albert Hall and speak at a rally on United Nations Day.' Kakia laughed.

'If it had been only that,' he said, not laughing at all. 'But she left me behind and said she'd come back. I waited and waited. You only seem to be able to get out of the place through Yugoslavia and then only once in a blue moon. She never replied to cables. I don't even know if she got them. She'd left her ticket in a book she lent me so I'd discovered it was only one-way, but I still thought she'd be coming back somehow. I couldn't believe it. God, I was slow. She's picked up some layabout in New York and Albania was a good place to park me. Well, I tracked her down. Isn't it obvious? Masquerading as her son. Good luck and good night.' His speech was unrecognisable; it seemed to have flown apart.

She took him up to his bedroom and gave him the last of his *marc*. When he had calmed down she told him about Harry and the usual transformation took place. He became collected, sane and devoted. 'We'll go out to dinner. You'll stay the night. Then tomorrow we'll fly back to London.

We should picket the Obstetricians and Gynaecologists. All right then, the Royal Society of Medicine. Has anyone ever done that? We should do something derisive. What about the girl? Someone must interview her on television.'

'She's having a nervous breakdown.'

'That's incriminating.'

'It's not because of the baby, it's because of Harry. I've seen her.'

'Well, she must be used to say so. That's crucial. Otherwise she's a very dangerous piece of evidence.'

'I know that. But she's not in a fit state yet.'

'Yes she is. I'll do it myself.'

He did need projects. He was very unlike Harry. She thought for a few moments of the idea of Don in prison, alone with himself with nothing to do. It would probably finish him. But then he was very unlikely ever to arrive there. And for him to court the idle slaughters of Christabel by loving her was perhaps as difficult a thing for him as an abortion for Harry.

XII

My darling,

I'm sitting at your desk. *Aida* is on at the opera house and a man in a dinner jacket has come into Broad Court to do something to his braces. He's taken his jacket off and standing there holding it and his wife's satin stole while she looks in her bag. I think he's lost a button. They look rather nice. He had a red beard like the one you sprouted. You might try it again, it worked rather well. They've got the road up in the Strand and I can just hear the drill still at it. It sounds different in the heat and quite soothing, like aeroplanes, You must be living in a crypt. I imagine you sitting quietly not moving very much. It's a good thing you don't fidget. I can't believe you're not here. Somebody asked me today why I was on my own at the pictures and when I told him where you were I felt as if I were telling some sort of fib. I don't go out much because I don't like the idea of you imagining me here and being wrong. I'm taking two months off to go down to the cottage, so write the next letter there.

I want to try to do some work that's a bit different. I can't manage deadlines at the minute. Your patients talk. about you endlessly. It's very gratifying and touching. I can't keep away from them. It's like a lot of photographs of you that I've never seen. I'm sleeping on your side of the bed. I love you with all my heart. Don't worry about anything. It's all waiting for you.

K.

Wandsworth
June 10th 1960

Darling,

It's the anniversary of the *wagon-lit*. I keep remembering what you looked like when I found you asleep in the corridor. I wonder why I didn't feel shy and go away. There's absolutely no news and the weather is awful here. I tried making a joke to myself about coming in to get away from the misery of the English summer but then I remembered you'd said it was sunny. I didn't know I could ever miss anyone like this. I'd made a promise to myself not to say so to you, but how can I tell you anything else. I feel pumped up with the thought of you, like some energetic lion, and I meant to feel like a recluse or at any rate like someone in the army. Your letter was sweet and comforting but it sounded desolate and it makes me anxious about you. Also there weren't enough details. The people in Broad Court were good but what film was it you went to? *What sort of drawings* are you doing? How's Don? I know you're trying not to remind me of things I can't have but at the minute I'd rather. Perhaps one feels differently after a time, but in a way I hope not. I hate the idea of getting acclimatised to loss, it's like submitting to dying. You'd make the most beautiful angry widow. You would have to go to Paris and blow a lot of money at Balenciaga.

Will you marry me?

H.

The Cottage
June 13th 1960

I can't believe it. It's the best idea possible. I was just leaving to go to the Post Office with a letter to you because I don't trust pillar-boxes with them, and then the postman came. How terrible if I'd already posted the other letter to you and you thought it meant I hadn't taken you seriously and you'd had to wait a whole week. The widow joke is unbearable. I'm writing this in Stroud post office very fast, which is a waste, but you must get it at once. There are two policemen in the next booth sending a very slow telegram wasting more words than me. The film was a Doris Day and she kept getting pregnant. You'd have liked it, that's why I saw it. I failed about an Ingmar Bergman but saw a beautiful old Buster Keaton. Some of it looked as if it was drawn. I feel about twenty-three. I've made a chart to tick off till you're out. I get a bit lonely here and also scared at night which I hadn't reckoned on but it makes a sort of contact with you sometimes. I went to Nice to tell Don about you, and Christabel had left him behind in Albania and disappeared. She'd made a speech in London and then scarpered to France and swears it was only to see her son, and now he seems to have decided to believe her. I don't know what she's at. Now she's persuaded her producer to let Don in on her next picture and he's over the moon and doesn't seem to know he's being fobbed off. It's painful to see and I try to imagine what you'd do about it. I've started wearing your shirts and sweaters. If the drawings are any good I'll try to describe them soon. I'm keeping the same hours as you. Being married makes it go a bit faster, I think.

K.

Each twenty-four hours without him had a cycle like the cycle of illness in hospital. If she had needed more sleep it would have been easier, but in spite of sleeping pills she found it impossible to quit consciousness for more than five or six hours, and even then slept guiltily as if she had dozed on guard. She woke as if she were falling, sometimes shouting at something. As the day went on it became more tolerable and she found tricks of mastering it. She read a book a day, every afternoon, and drew all morning and again early in the evening. Some of her drawings were libellous centaur fables about the men who had punished Harry. She drew the lawyers and medical dignitaries with the bodies of asses and hyenas, guffawing together and drinking. Harry's local vicar, who had attacked him in the parish magazine and been picked up and supported in a right-wing tabloid, was a thick cob hunting him down in a field of Roman Catholic cardinals barnacled with jewellery. The Home Secretary, listening to a question in the House of Lords as she had seen him, was sprawled on the red carpeted stairs behind the Woolsack like a man at a picnic, but with pigs' trotters coming out of his trousers. She started using colour washes, especially a green that was like the liquid around English processed peas and a bilious yellow like sodium street lighting, with deep magenta bags under the eyes of heavily made-up women baying after pregnant unmarried girls.

At the same time she was starting to do something quite different and trying to draw pornography. She had often wondered if it was really true that women didn't respond to sex in art and felt more and more sure that it wasn't. She worked swiftly and simply; the drawings were unpublishable, jubilant and very erotic, She thought that some of them might be good.

In September Don began plaguing her to come up to Scotland to see him on the location of Christabel's film. She was back in London at work, and had to say in the end that she would go.

Don had never written a film before. He was plainly at odds with the leading man, a tanned boy with a pop-Cockney accent born and brought up in Liverpool, who had been cast before Don came onto the picture. Christabel seemed to like Don's feelings for her to be made as public as possible and talked intimacies to him in front of the film crew. On the first day she took to saying 'This won't interest you' to Kakia whenever conversation turned to some practical matter, as though she had at sometime announced a taste against action, like a dislike of a particular food.

'This won't interest you, of course,' she said sympathetically at dinner in their dim hotel when the cameraman had been talking about a lens.'

'Why ever not?'

Christabel went on smiling. 'What news of Harry?' she said. 'He's a doctor,' she explained to the leading man, who was called Hug Aitchbone, presumably not by his parents. 'He went to prison for doing an abortion, poor darling. It's the most dreadful thing.' In her piping choirboy voice the words had the ring of a destructive fact of history recited by a school-pet who was at the very least too young for it, if not about to sneak.

Hug had just been to America and brought back for Christabel a tortoise that he had had fitted up with a private-eye's tape recorder. The recorder was the size of a jewel and embedded into its shell. The evil living gag clambered wretchedly around the table for a while, baffled by its extra weight and veering helplessly to the left with its head slowly waving like a pterodactyl's.

'What have you had done to it?' said Kakia.

'It's bugged,' said Nick.

'What's that?'

He shrugged.

Don said: 'When you switch it on to play back the poor creature goes out of its mind with the racket. I'm not going to have it.' By then Kakia had understood what bugged meant.

'Darling, you're being RSPCA again,' said Christabel. 'It doesn't know a thing. They wouldn't allow it if it was painful.'

Don looked at her and picked up the tortoise and tried to dismantle something, but he could never do anything with his hands. Hug looked at him without expression. The match between them was fixed by nature from the start. Don fought his life on the ground of being the new man, and now there was a newer new man on the other side of the table who made Don's own coolness seem comparatively flailing and his zest due for extinction. Don was suggestible, clever, accident-prone and extravagant; Hug was dispassionate, efficient, with the infallibility of the unconcerned and the stinginess of the man who cherishes nothing. Christabel seemed to have studied him as though he were some sort of course in modernity, and explained him earnestly while he tinkered with the tortoise.

'Hug does an hour's judo every morning. Isn't it enterprising? Even when he's filming. He's got a black-belt. There are hardly any black-belts outside Japan. When he's not filming he runs a personal relations agency. That's the modern sort of public relations. He says a lot of people in Liverpool think he's freakish but that he's only ahead of his time. He believes in getting across people because if you don't care about them there isn't a thud when they drop you. I thought that was rather cynical but he says the great thing is to be honest. I'm going to convert him to politics if it kills me. He's so unpolitical it's like being colour-blind. Of course the trouble is he can't remember the war. He's so young he makes Don and me feel a hundred and eight.' She lent right over the table and kissed Don on his nose. Hug started doing things with a nail-file, first to the tortoise and then to his nails. It was as if he were being subtitled, and he seemed to enjoy it mildly, if he really enjoyed anything at all, for it was difficult to imagine him entertaining any hunger that was not instantly satisfiable or any yearning intense enough to plague him. He seemed to feed himself on demand; when they sat down to dinner he joined them in nothing, because he had been hungry half an hour before and eaten a sandwich.When he did eventually speak, Kakia saw why it was that Christabel had fallen into this way of talking about him; he made exactly the same sort of dislocated pronouncements about himself. During the evening he made not one answer, put no questions, and said nothing that attached to what anyone else was talking about. Christabel thought she was doing things for him that he welcomed as signs of love; but he treated them more like the unwanted extra helpings that mothers will often pile onto affronted grown men's plates in the hope of winning back the dependence of infancy.

'We'll try to instruct Hug,' she said gaily over the brackish little cups of coffee in the television lounge. 'Don is, what shall we say you are? I think you're a systematised Tory anarchist. Kakia is a lapsed Polish Fabian.'

'Who have you been talking to?' said Kakia. 'Compared with you I'm as red as a boiled lobster.'

'You're always complaining about the Russians and censorship and things.'

'I hate games like this. Please let's stop.'

'Aren't you?'

'Hating censorship isn't anti-Left. Censorship isn't confined to Communist countries. What about Algeria? We had it between the wars in Poland. You've got it here. I've just done some drawings that could never be published here.'

'What, political drawings?'

'The ones I meant are obscene.'

'Political censorship's more important. We haven't got that.'

'If so, then maybe it's only because you care about it less. But if someone wrote a play showing how Tory the monarchy really is, or a farce about the Queen being shoved out to Quebec to hold Canada together and getting riddled with Republican bullets when she really wants to be at home riding in a gymkhana, do you think it would be allowed?'

'I don't understand you. Why did you leave Poland, then? If people like you had stayed, you might have been able to make Gomulka a real triumph. Darling Hug, do you want me to tell you who Gomulka is? He took over the Polish Communists in 1956 and stood up to Khrushchev and nearly got Poland free.'

'I do judo to keep my mind fit,' said Hug. 'I'm the brightest I know. I've no wish to disguise the fact that I have a fantastic ego.'

'Would you like to rehearse?' said Don.

Kakia said: 'Christabel, I'm in England because it suits *me*, but you wouldn't suit *Poland*. You can't try to make everywhere else just like here. Poland may hate Russia but it couldn't want anything but socialism now. Why do you always assume that Poland and Hungary and everywhere else are struggling underneath to be a sort of Catholic England or a miniature America?'

'At least we don't lock people up who disagree,' said Christabel.

'I hope Harry heard that in his cell,' said Don.

'I treat women as a commodity,' said Hug with a flicker of interest in himself. 'If it's beautiful I'll have it. Yuh, that's right. I'm pretty generous. I give them things and that puts them on my side. I make them like I make films. Four a year. I just turn them out, and if they're no good I'm not bothered. I'm talking about girls.'

'You see what I mean about honesty,' said Christabel.

'I really would like to talk about the script,' said Don.

'Hug hates planning, darling. He's much more himself when he improvises.'

'The rushes today were a balls up.'

'When I direct a film,' said Hug, 'I'm going to do it off the top of my head.'

'People should only do that when they've made a lot of films,' said Kakia. 'And when they've got actors like Christabel who know what they're doing. It sounds an arrogant way to begin.'

'He's not an amateur, sweetheart. He's made four films and dozens of commercials and personal appearances.'

'You and I could do some work alone together, then,' said Don to Christabel. He brightened up greatly and took her away to his room with the script. Kakia talked to the cameraman for a while and then went out for a walk. They were in a sheltered part of Scotland, and the air was sweet and balmy. In the loch below there was a girl water-skiing behind a motorboat, along the track of a lamp that was like a searchlight on a police launch. She was on a mono-ski and looked miraculous. Kakia went back to the hotel and wrote a letter.

September 19th 1960

My darling,

I'm in Scotland on Don's location. A beautiful girl has just gone along the loch on one ski. Braced right back. She looked like a charioteer. I wish I could do any such thing. It's like some of *Così*. I love you with all my heart. I know I must, and how good a man you are, because anything hard to do always makes me think of you.

Kakia.

Before she went to bed Don asked her to come out for a drink at the pub.

'What about Christabel?'

'She's gone to bed.'

'Shouldn't you? What time do you get up?'

'Half-past five or six. I'm too keyed up.'

They had a brandy in a pub that had leaflets about sheep auctions on the counter. Kakia had an impression that Don was struggling to carpenter something beyond his powers out of a plot that could never be anything but factitious. She wished she could lower the pressure of his excitement about it.

'Did you tell Harry about Paris?' he said suddenly.

'Yes.'

He was very angry.

'I'm so sorry. I'd no idea you wouldn't want him to know. Well: yes, I see it, of course I do now. I'm really very sorry! He wanted to know how you were.'

'You should have left me to tell him.'

'You can. I've hardly said anything at all.'

'*What* have you said?'

'Wait. I must try to get it right. I think it was that she'd left you behind in Albania, spoken at a rally and then gone off to Paris with someone she said was her son. That was all.'

'Thank you very much. I suppose you've told him all about us too.'

'What there was to know he knew himself. We weren't invisible.'

'I think Christabel was telling the truth in Nice. I think she's just casual; I don't think she's promiscuous.'

'Would it wreck everything for you if she were?'

'In principle no, but in fact I'm afraid it might. Like everyone else, I suppose. I can't stand the idea of you blabbing to Harry. How could you? I thought I could trust you.'

'I've done no such thing. Nothing. You mustn't believe such things. You shouldn't assume that everyone you love is hell-bent on betraying you. You're trying to pretend I'm Christabel, aren't you? You should be saying these things to her.'

He started a cigarette. 'Just because you don't like her.'

'Sometimes I do. I don't really have very much feeling about her except in relation to you.'

'I'm absolutely crazy about her, you know.'

'I know.' Yet he didn't seem happy. He was in the grip of a love that was like jealousy, and she could see there was no rest in it anywhere. It was like being in a cell where the light was never turned off and he could neither sit nor stand nor lie.

When she was taking her make-up off at the wash-basin Kakia heard a couple at it in Christabel's room next door and realised what she had known subconsciously all along.

If she came away from the wall their voices faded but they were still intelligible. She went out into the corridor but couldn't tell which of the doors was Don's; there was one opposite that might be his, but also one on the other side of Christabel's. She prayed that at least their bed was on her wall and not on the opposite one that might be Don's.

'What've you done with the tortoise I gave you?' said Hug's voice.

'Oh. I think I left it downstairs,' said Christabel.

'Lovely recording of vacuum cleaning there'll be tomorrow morning. If you ever find it, that is.'

'Darling.'

'I don't give presents to have them thrown away.'

'I'll go and find it, shall I?'

'Better get on with it. I've got to get to sleep.'

The next five minutes passed very slowly.

Then Christabel said: 'You do care for me, don't you?'

'What am I wearing tomorrow?'

'I don't remember.'

'I'm going to wear my own clothes. I just decided. They don't know how I dress on this picture. Ties. I don't wear ties. I wear a dark shirt, bottle maybe, or navy, or dark red but not a mauvy red, with matching buttons, and that's it. Very neat, and nice and short. They always make a shirt too long, you got to stuff it round your crutch like a nappy. I mean I don't use my arms, so it's not as if it'll pull out will it? I'm not a manual worker, am I? Only thing I do is take off my guitar or put it on, and when I do that then I can be careful. It's a question of having your belt nice and tight. If it's a good belt your shirt don't pull out. In America they've got a belt now that's got burrs on the back. Burrs. Something like a thistle. You get a beautiful grip. I got three of them.'

'I do love you without a tie.'

'Why do you think all those nits from Eton have shirts down to their knees? *They're* not manual workers.

I shouldn't think they lift their arms all day. Course the trouble is they wear braces. If you wear braces the weight is from your shoulders and there's no grip round your waist so your shirt's bound to pull up. Still, they could have twelve inches off and not be worried.

They don't know how to dress, course.'

'I think you look wonderful – You look like Clark Gable.'

'Who?'

'Apart from the moustache, I meant. I suppose I really, meant you've got the same body. Your face isn't alike at all, I mean. I don't suppose you'd want to look like Clark Gable, would you?'

'I'm not fussy. What's he look like?'

'Darling, what a wonderful remark. Everyone else in the film industry is so competitive. It's a sort of woodworm. You just don't care about them, do you? It's something to be very proud of?

'Did I tell you about the time I went to the Café de Pan's a few years ago? They told me it was the last thing. Marlene Dietrich and all that. You know who I mean. Thin blonde, knows a lot about a mike. Well, I roll up and I'm in my first Bentley. I got a chauffeur, course, all in uniform, perfectly correct. And I'm wearing a new medium dark blue Italian silk suit, something between a royal and a navy, and a beautiful ruffled shirt that cost the earth, you could have got married in it. And shoes with a nice point made in Rome and very fine wool socks because nylon makes my feet sweat, pardon me, and now comes the punch line. No tie. Well, it's my trade mark. That's how I dress. I even got gold cuff links in the shape of a guitar my bird gone and give me. My current bird. Well: I send the chauffeur off and tell him I'll be a couple of hours. And then, do you mind, they won't let me in and say I'm not properly dressed. I had a shout up but it didn't do no good. All it did was give me a terrible headache. I had to go to the all-night chemist and get something. They wouldn't let me in. Would you believe it. And I'd sent the car away. I could have murdered them. What had they got in there but a lot of car salesmen and Jewish hairdressers?'

'And you'd come all the way from Liverpool.'

'It wasn't that. I was staying at the Savoy. But I'd sent the car away. And Christ I got a headache.'

'Darling, do you want an aspirin?'

'Not *now*. I mean I had a headache then. You've got to clean your ears out.'

'Sweetheart don't think about it.'

'I'll do that place one day.'

'Isn't it closed?'

'If it isn't I'll close it.'

'You do love me, don't you?'

'I told you, don't get tangled up. I haven't got time for other people any more than I've got time for myself or else I'd end up as a garage mechanic.'

'I feel quite different with you.'

'Mind you, I've nothing special against garage mechanics. I just don't want to be one.'

'Darling, don't go. It's awful to leave each other.'

'Got my alarm there. Anyway I can't sleep except on my own.'

'Yes you can. I'll make it lovely. Don always gets up and goes. Don't remind me.'

'What's he like in bed?'

'You shouldn't ask that.'

'All right, don't answer. I was only being polite.'

There was a short pause. 'He doesn't know what he's doing. He's all over the place, poor darling. He's all legs. It's like going to bed with a deckchair that keeps folding up. It's the same as the way he walks.'

'Like this?'

'That's very cruel.' But she laughed. 'You're quite a good actor, aren't you. If you try.'

'It's a crappy picture. Why bother?'

'For the sake of your own self-esteem, at least for that.'

There was a pause. 'For me, then.'

'Listen. You got a script that's a load of cod's wollop, a director that's your own very personal mistake, an old-hat posh actress to pull in the class and me for the kids. That's it, isn't it? Those are the items.'

There was a sob like a man's, but it couldn't have been his.

'That's what you've got. Why kill yourself?'

'It's important to me. Our time together, our film, every thing. I know it isn't to you but I swear it is to me. Would I be doing this if it wasn't? It's the most important thing in my life for at least ten years. The last ten years.' Again she sobbed, like a man, and it was strange and unforgettable that it should be so unlike her voice. 'I've been drifting. It's all been going away from me. You don't know how different I feel when we're on the set. Working together. And here. It's like a little home. Playing houses.'

'Oh blimey.' There was a pause, and someone's feet on the floor. 'Listen. Just don't be a drag. I think you're very nice. Right? You're very nice in bed. Right? It suits me.

I hope it suits you. But if it don't that's too bad. Ok?'

'Yes. Of course you're absolutely right. You make everything seem so simple. That's what I like about you. No strings. That's what you mean, isn't it?' All night Kakia heard her sobbing every now and then, the terrible man's sob that is quite dry and comes not from the throat but the guts!

Next morning Kakia was woken at seven-thirty and there was a car to take her to the location. Don was wearing dark glasses and she couldn't decipher his expression. They were rehearsing a scene in a sitting-room. When Hug and Christabel appeared Don seemed to have taken over from the director completely and told them sharply to get on to the sofa.

'We're going to improvise. Right. I'll give you the situation. Forget the script. You're thirty-eight and fed up with an old affair. You're twenty and she's around. He's given you a present and you've forgotten it somewhere.' The two started to try to invent, but they were like drugged people and nothing happened. So Don gave them their lines from the night before, one by one, exactly as Kakia had heard them. When it was over Hug said with a trace of interest:

'Did you have the tortoise turned on?'

'No.' Don took off his glasses and looked at him with dry command. 'There are times when people have total recall.'

What was to make him suffer most later, in a torment nearly beyond tolerance, was Christabel's phlegm. The scene was better than anything else he had written and he grimly made the director edit it to use in the picture, which meant running it over and over again. Her performance was without courage, lacking either hardship or distress. All it had was nerve.

Part Three

XIII

Kakia met Harry outside Wandsworth Prison at seven-thirty in the morning. He was carrying his head as if he were afraid of spilling it, which meant that he had a migraine. The inner door in the huge entrance gate opened like a trap-door for cats, and he stepped out carefully without looking down because of his head. He had gone in with clothes that were as inflammatory as possible and he looked like a dandy drawn by Beerbohm. She was wearing a new orange coat for much the same reason, and a fur beret. 'You look beautiful,' he said. 'Like Anna Karenina your face has got so thin.'

They got into the car and then she took her coat off and he saw that she was six or seven months pregnant.

'You're not joking? It is real?'

Then he went out of his mind with joy.

'Why didn't you tell me?'

'I was so frightened we'd lose it. We nearly did three times. It's all right now. The first time was after I went up to Don in Scotland on location and I didn't even know I was pregnant.'

'I thought people only did that when they'd had thirteen children. Now know, I mean. How could you not know?'

'I thought I was just out of gear because of missing you and being low and not eating. It happened in the war.'

'I had an instinct, last time but one, but it was only your face. You were all bundled up in a coat. It was just an instinct and it vanished. My darling, you've got far too thin.'

They drove away. Don too had come to meet him, without Kakia knowing it, but he had loitered at the gates and when he saw what was going on he stole away in his hired car. He was full of what are called mixed feelings, as the deeper ones perhaps always are. He felt happiness and at the same time a stab of mortality. He had a very strong sense that he could be free of thoughts of Christabel now that Harry was out, and yet at the same time he had another quite distinct sense that something immeasurably sad was happening. At the moment when Harry was feeling such an intensity of life that he could hardly bear the pang that it brought, Don was noticing how grey his hair was, and thinking of his own, which was changing too, and feeling stricken by the spectacle of his dear friend aged and spent, who was now embarking on a life that could only spend him a little more. He felt melancholy and quizzical, and for a few moments quite unlike himself. Never give in. But never give in to what?

Growing incredulous of his efforts to deceive himself, Don tried to get others to deceive him. Instead of making up his own emphatic quick solutions and forming them like epigrams, he lost his nerve for it and started quoting only the sayings of the celebrated people he was drawn to. His new sense of growing older, which salted his other wounds, could be allayed only by seeing the young and the impeccably in touch. He took their scathing effect on him to be his own fault. Once he had thought of himself as being a master of his period; now he felt he had lost the sense of it, like some knack, or being in love. He could hear his voice repeating the shrill theoretical enthusiasms of a thousand straw prophets, and reproducing the knockabout derision that was the new piety. He began to mix with people whose ethic was to be as neutral as possible; it was close enough to his own lifelong disguise of objectivity to attract him, and the lack of anything debonair in it was a secret deprivation that he never dared to put his finger on. The fact that these people depleted him, made him feel practically cancelled out, could only be his own fault for not being cool enough, he thought. He blamed himself, in fact, for not being like the nerveless boy in Christabel's bed.

He changed the hotel where he lived and went to a new hairdresser, leaving the one that he and Harry had shared for years because Harry's life and tastes were now too unattainable a model to do anything but irk him. He still admired him and would like to emulate the result of the way he lived, but the process of it was something he shrank from. The seclusion of it, the apparent contentment to be doing nothing in particular, the easy way that he and Kakia lived together on what she earned, struck Don simultaneously as inconsequential, a little splendid, pointless, incomparable and anyway quite beyond his own reach. He worked more and more in television and became a casting director in the theatre, for which he had a flair. Overwork became the only ethic he would support. A magazine that was doing a feature on holidays interviewed him as the obligatory plain speaker of the early 1960's; he said that work was the only thing in life and that Sammy Davis Junior said that holidays were responsible for more unhappiness than heroin. In fact Don had said this himself, but quoting others had become a nervous habit. Kakia saw the magazine before Harry did and concealed it from him because both of them had already worried about whether Don really enjoyed spending time off with them any longer. Though he still asked himself down to stay with them, he seemed restless to be doing nothing and obscurely agitated by the sight of them.

One day, when Kakia's twins were about nine months old, Don had a letter from Christabel.

Darling Don,

You were sweet enough to send me on my clothes and the scripts and things. I'm afraid I leave a lot of stuff everywhere, don't I? I've been meaning to write for ages but I expect you've seen how busy I've been. Somebody gave me a scarab brooch the other day and it says on it 'Time passes' in Arabic. I thought it was rather sad. Did I leave my charm bracelet behind? If so could your secretary send it?

Love,

C.

It was an attempt, perhaps. And yet it meant nothing to him. He had kept the charm bracelet but his life had left it and he sent it back, posting it in a pipesmoker's matchbox from the Charing Cross Road Post Office one evening when he had been at a theatre in St Martin's Lane with a brassy girlfriend.

XIV

Really one of the reasons why he still went to stay at the cottage was to let rip his rumbling conservatism and his passion for running things, which were both thwarted by the company he kept. He came down one weekend a while later armed with a girl whom he seemed to treat as a sort of parking meter, feeding her drinks and meals like sixpences in return for the right to draw up there. She was quite silent and very cool, dressed in a schoolboy's blazer, grey flannel shorts and white knee socks. She was obviously surprised to find herself in the country and had apparently never before been in a house that had a baby in it, but her coolness stopped her saying so. She had dimples on her knees which were rather touching, and a disconcerting habit of winking with first one eye and then the other. Neither Harry nor Kakia was able to decide whether this was involuntary or a piece of friendliness. It was an odd sort of wink for a girl, very heavy, like the wink that is made in a commercial by a milkman or a policeman after he has told you that you're on to a good thing if you drink milk or that it's a great life in the police force.

Don parked her in a chair and said to Kakia in an attacking voice:

'Why aren't you and Harry married?'

'We couldn't get married when I was seven months pregnant.'

'Plenty of people do it.'

'Bad reason.'

'Why aren't you married? I thought you were going to.'

This was a technique: to rephrase with a quite spurious mournfulness, something that she hoped had already been answered, so that her second reply was lamer and more defensive than the first.

'Having children put me off a bit. Not off *Harry*. Off getting married.' He declined to understand. 'It would have been different if we'd done it before I was pregnant.'

He still demanded something more. 'I daresay we will when they're older. They're too young to get any fun out of it.

'You're being very selfish and silly.'

'What on earth does it matter? Getting married's something between the two of us. It's neither here nor there to anyone else.'

'It will be to your children at school'

'Whatever sort of school do you think they're going to?'

'What sort of school *are* they going to go to?'

Kakia said sullenly, feeling that no good was ever going to come of this conversation: 'The local here, I hope. Or wherever. Or perhaps I'll teach them. Or Harry.'

'Isn't Harry ever going to do a job again?'

'He hasn't had any time to read for years,' she said.

Harry had been feeling strongly for some time that he should be saying something.

'I haven't had any time to read for years, you see,' he said after thinking about it, and then heard the echo of it in his eardrum. This was as much as he could manage with Don in his present mood. Suddenly all conversation seemed impossible and absurd; nobody having the right amount of nerve at the right time, people tracking backwards and forwards over the same idea like lawn mowers, picking each other up for things they hadn't meant and refraining from saying all the things that they most badly wanted other people to know. Kakia saw the difficulty and dropped him a cue. 'We need a spot of cheering up,' she said, meaning a whisky, and he himself cheered up insitantly. When they were by themselves they had taken to drinking South African sherry mixed with soda water and ice because it was cheap and not at all bad, but they had some whisky for the days when Don came. Actually the Scotch had run out and they had forgotten to get any more, and all they had was half a bottle of Bols that they had bought for a Dutch girlfriend of them both who had run away from her husband and sheltered with them for a few days with her three children and a frosty Lutheran nanny. But when their friend arrived she had turned out only to like English gin, so the idea was not as welcoming as they had wanted it to be.

'What's that?' said Don.

'It's not bad with a lot of ice. It's Bols.' It was a ridiculous word for an Englishman and extremely difficult to say like a host. Don had a sip and left the rest.

'Would she like an orange squash?' said Kakia, about the girl.

'I think she'd rather have a coke.'

Then Kakia wondered why on earth she had offered an orange squash, for they didn't even possess such a thing. She suddenly realised that it must be because of the girl's clothes, which had made her quite seriously start to think of her as a small English schoolboy.

'Would you like a coke?' she said, for it really was very rude not to talk to her directly, although Don seemed to talk about her like this as well. The question was clearly ludicrous. 'Would you like a coke,' indeed. As if it were half-term. And Kakia didn't even generally use the word; she said 'Coca-Cola.' It sounded at once like the most grovelling attempt to be young. 'Would you like a Coca-Cola?'

The girl nodded and winked on both sides. It was like a signal turning round all night on an airport tarmac. Perhaps the winking really was intentional, and the whole thing struck her as funny; for which Kakia couldn't blame her at all. But the offer was academic because there wasn't any Coca-Cola either, and why should there be in a cottage inhabited by the two of them and a pair of baby twins? So she produced an infant's concentrated orange juice frappe, and the girl loved it and had another. As the weekend went on she turned out to have a passion for 'the babies' rose hip syrup, which she must have seen in the bathroom, for she started helping herself to it and finished the lot. So then the babies had water and sugar instead.

'She looks awfully cold,' said Harry when they were alone. He was talking about Don's girlfriend; the children were fine. 'Do you think the cottage's warm enough?'

'Perhaps it's because she doesn't move about.'

'Nor do we.'

'No, nor do we.'

'Other people's houses always feel colder,' said Harry.

'But that natural sugar should be warming, shouldn't it? A whole bottle and a half of rose hip. Shall I offer her a sweater? We'll put all the heaters on in their room.'

On Sunday morning the girl came down into the little low-roofed sitting-room looking just as chilly, although the bedroom had been boiling when Kakia had taken in their breakfast. It was something to do with her white make-up and not wearing lipstick, perhaps. To Kakia's surprise the girl suddenly spoke and asked if she could take the twins out for a walk in the pram. When they came back two hours later the babies both looked fascinated and dropped off to sleep in the warm indoors as if concussed.

'Did they behave?' Kakia asked.

'We had a nice time. They're sweet. You've no idea. Trusting me with your *babies*. What it means.' She started to cry and then did the washing-up and sang *I've Got You Under My Skin*.

'You know what it is. She's longing to have a baby and doesn't like to ask anyone for one,' said Kakia to Harry.

'I thought they didn't mind asking that sort of thing.'

'They don't mind the sex but I don't think she can face the talking.'

They had a large lunch very late. Don had been to the pub

and bought them a crate of drink. He always hated being thanked and carried it in as if it were nothing to do with him. Kakia clung to him with relief for a few moments and then looked at him and said:

'We mustn't go on at Harry about what he's going to do.'

'Why can't he go on with medicine? Other people do it when they're off the register.'

'He thinks it wouldn't be quite fair.'

'Why?'

'He says that when you're having a baby you've got to be confident, and perhaps if someone was in pain they wouldn't be.'

'I see that,' he said.

'I haven't heard you say that for ages.'

'What do you think he should do, then?'

'Wait, I think. Give himself some air and not be hustled. I don't know. I think he might do research or teach. He's reading American history at the moment. Not for any reason. He says he hadn't thought of it before but nobody in England ever gets taught anything about it.'

They planned to have dinner very late. Kakia and Harry were in their bedroom reading and the girl twin was lying down looking severely at her feet. The boy was asleep as usual. He slept whenever they put him down, like a tramp.

'Right. What's penosis?' said Kakia.

'Penosis is –' I'll tell you. This is a very interesting word that people often get wrong.'

'You're playing for time. You don't know. I'll tell you.'

'You didn't give me a chance.'

'It's the ebbing of joy after meals.'

'Oh yes, that is good. That's brilliant. You've found something that never had a name. Yes. And there are places in the world where penosis is supposed not to exist. Where people go to escape from it. But it follows them, to sunny places and Muslim places and famous gastronomic restaurants and anywhere at all, and once you've felt penosis you're never sure you can be free of it again, like malaria. Like *post coitum omne animale triste sunt* or whatever it is. Penosis is *post prandia omni homini*, can't remember what meal is, *cena*, is it? *Cenus. Cibus.*'

'Darling, I've no idea what you're talking about.'

'I thought you spoke every language there was.'

'Not Latin. That is Latin, isn't it? I didn't even go to school after I was thirteen.'

'I always forget.'

'What does it mean, anyway?'

'That man is the only animal that feels sad after fucking.'

'I don't. After *meals*, yes. Do other people really feel sad? How – sad. But then I didn't have the post-baby sadness either, did I? I think I got it all done when I was pregnant and luckily I couldn't inflict it on you then.'

'That girl of Don's looks proper parky to me. What is her name?'

'Oh no she isn't, she's sweet. Susan. She said she doesn't like being called Sue, or Susie – or Su-su, so she said, whoever would do that.'

'Darling, parky means cold.'

'I thought it meant nasty.'

'No, that's narky. Or sarky. I know more English than you at last. What's Russian for lick my boots?'

'Wait a minute. I can't remember lick.'

'Well, say eat.'

She laughed. 'I can only say eat my galoshes. Galoshes make me think of Chekhov. How nice. Do you know he left a fragment on a bit of paper after he died and it said "If you cry 'Forward!' you must without fail explain in which direction." That's absolutely the only tone of voice that sounds to me genuinely serious about politics any longer and it's a great help to bear in mind when Don's going on at anyone about

Capitalism or Communism or something. If you see everyone charging equally hard in equally wrong directions all shouting Progress with their fingers in the air – very earnestly – wanting the best most of the time – Is that book any good?'

'Why do you always want my book?' he said.

'The same reason that you always want mine, I suppose. Other people always seem to have a choice that's somehow more sure and serious and original than yours and your own seems fumbling and peripheral.'

'I don't feel that, actually. Do you feel it about other people's drawings?'

'Oh. No; I don't, not at all. Especially not if I'm drawing anything myself. Then I can't look at the good people anyway.'

'Who?'

'Oh. I can't do lists. Hogarth, Goya, Gillray, Grünewald, Dürer. Most of George Grosz. Often Ronald Searle, he draws beautifully. Vicky. Eight or ten people.'

XV

A while later, towards the end of 1962, Don had come down
to stay as usual with a different girl. Ambrose was there as
well, sleeping on the sofa, with the twins separated in Kakia's
bedroom and a cloakroom because they woke each other up.
Kakia and Harry had discovered. a long time ago, as people do
who aren't strapped to nurses' rules, that if you wake babies up
at twelve or one before you go to bed yourself and exhaust them
with activity and food instead of waiting for them to exhaust
you at three or six in the morning, they will often sleep happily
until nine or ten. It was Saturday night at one-thirty in the
morning and the girl baby was tottering cheerfully about the
room hooting with laughter at Don, whom she found funny,
which he resented, and playing a game with Ambrose about
pulling out his wallet. The boy seemed to be nodding off.

'Hey, give him the radio,' said Harry. The baby liked the radio
and seemed to think he was playing it rather well, like an
instrument.

'It's much too late for them,' said Don.

'They love it. It's like going to the theatre for them. It's surely
much nicer to be woken up to have fun and wear yourself out
than to wake up all alone and scream,' said Kakia.

'Babies need lots of sleep.'

'Well, they get lots of sleep, but these two get some of it at the
same time as us instead of the same time as the birds.'

'You just brought them out and I didn't know you had
them,' said Don's present girl, who spoke more than the others
usually did.

'I could do a study of taste on the basis of Don's girls,' said Ambrose in the kitchen. 'This one is the backcombing chapter. Have girls who read books completely gone out?'

'Don't you suppose she does?'

'I know she doesn't. I've spoken to her. I'm quite sure she hasn't got a thing to read in her flat apart from a bullfight calendar.'

'What happened about the job?' said Don after dinner.

'I've decided to do it,' said Harry. To his great surprise, he had been offered a teaching post by a new university. 'I've come to the conclusion it's not charity. They're not kind enough for that. And the students looked rather good.'

'But you won't be able to manage about the twins,' Don said. Why was it, that he seemed to resent the idea of their lives not being particularly hampered by children?

'We'll be able to afford someone to help. And if she's not there Kakia can do it, or if Kakia's not there I can do it. It works out all right. What you do is decide you're living with them all day and do the pottering and chatting then, though you can always take it in turns to read and go out, and then they shut up in the evening. I am being boring, I'm sorry.'

'I don't think you'll find it as easy as all that.' Don sometimes sounded like a matron. Harry saw him very clearly: tall and handsome, with a tight starched belt, a tower of strength to the medical staff, and absolutely detested by patients trying to recover from a stroke or struggling to walk. He wondered if he was ever going to have a chance to talk seriously to him again. For months he had known that he was unhappy, but Don created edgy conditions now in which it was impossible to mention it. Bantering and mock hostility had become a habit, and there was always one of his girls there to prevent Harry risking a confrontation. The girls were different every time he came down and they gave him not only a sexual alibi before Harry but also a means of protection. He had grown good at using their presence to allow himself to talk always a little facetiously, as other people will sometimes use their children to develop a habit of speaking that is without ambiguity and more emphatic than they mean it to be. Don was derisive about any responses that were at all complicated, as he was about any talk of feelings. Christabel seemed to have sickened him of emotionalism forever, including his own. What he insisted on were facts, and opinions expressed with inhuman neatness. These he was happy to play with as though they were a sort of soap bubble in the air for anyone to blow in any direction, instead of the extension of a personality. The brilliant, ambitious, uselessly self-knowing man had remade himself again; long ago Harry had admired him for being self-constructed, but he kept suspecting now with dread in his heart that the new model arose from nothing but agitation and that it pleased even the inventor very little.

As Harry and Kakia had known him, Don's soft-heartedness had seemed indestructible; but now he started concealing it and played barbaric games, inventing fantasies about professional humiliation for famous people and tests to find flaws in his friends which he chortled at with no particular enjoyment. Harry tried again and again to engage him in talking about himself but the knife kept slipping off the bone.

'Did you tell Harry about Christabel in Scotland?' he said to Kakia once.

'Yes, I'm afraid I did. I remembered the row we had about telling him about Nice but when I thought about it later I thought I was right after all. It's not gossip when it's to Harry. You must remember that both times you'd asked me to be there. In the telephone box and on location. When I tried to go you wouldn't let me. I wasn't there by accident.'

He said then, with more hatred than she had ever heard in someone she liked: 'Telling that story is worse than inventing it.'

Yet when he talked to Harry some time after, with a girl parked as usual in a chair like a dog, he made a knowing reference to the Christabel scene as it stood in the film and laughed his new harsh laugh, which was like a chisel drawn across cement, and within himself experienced some thankfulness that Harry had a key to his feelings, for he could not for the life of him any longer have expressed them himself.

'An irregular polygamy is the ideal,' he said fiercely. His girl didn't even cower.

The other two didn't react either, so he tried a needle in the other flank. 'Monogamy is a product of the instinct of property.'

'Yes and no,' said Harry, grinning. 'Like most things you say. Or what I suppose I mean is yes *but*. True, but what else. Have a drink.'

'The Judaic-Christian tradition of monogamy is based on an idea of fidelity not as a good but as goods.'

'Oh, darling,' said Kakia.

'What do you think it is?'

'Oh, Nebuchadnezzar, spinach, I don't know. Have a drink, Prue. You look bored to tears and you're quite right.'

'What about?' said Prue, safely switched off.

'You must have decided what you think,' said Don to Kakia again. 'You make each other believe in it, apparently.' He laughed. 'Do you really think it's workable? I think it's the most farcical bourgeois convention ever devised.'

Kakia did then try to reply. 'Monogamy's a brutal word. It should be constancy. Constancy's a structure for expressing something, that's all. A style, like an art. But nobody can ask you to be good at it. You can only offer it, and either you feel it or you don't. If you're fortunate it's possible.' She moved to the fire because she was in danger of crying for some reason. 'There's no need to obey it as a convention any longer, you see. If you do it's often a cruel one. Some people are trying to turn it into something else. It's not easy.'

Don looked at Kakia's profile. 'It's odd,' he said, 'that even when you're not talking you always look as if you're blowing something.'

'It's my upper lip.' She drew it cruelly into the steam on the window pane. 'My gibbon mouth.'

'Is *that* why you called yourself Gibbon? I thought it was because you saw yourself as an observer of history.'

'Oh, dear. I'm afraid I hadn't heard of him then. And now that's what people often assume and there's nothing I can do about it. I hardly went to school, you see. I don't really know anything at all. I know about what I've read and then there are suddenly great gaps about things that everyone else knows who's got any education at all.'

'Your drawings are getting more fierce and your character is getting more forgiving,' he said.

'Did you mean that nicely?' It had been said like an attack; she didn't know how to react.

'Yes.'

'Oh. I wish it were true.' She knew she hadn't been responsive, but the gesture had been made in a way that practically forbade it. If he would only make some sort of contact with Harry; but this seemed beyond possibility. Harry was looking unusually grim and she wondered if he thought she had been conciliatory.

'What do *you* think about the Common Market?' said Don to Harry, who shook his head.

'I've no idea,' he said.

'I'm living in America in 1832 at the minute.'

Ambrose was staying with them again and walked in from the garden, flailing his arms and stomping his feet against the cold like a cab-driver.

'What do *you* think about the Common Market?' Don asked him.

'I decided today that the appalling thing is I agree with Edward Heath. It's like agreeing with your mother.'

'Kakia thinks we should stay out of it, according to her drawings, because Barbara Castle's right and it's a rich club. Kakia, what do you really think?'

Ambrose sat by the fire with a drink. 'She once said to me that the thing that absolutely everybody can be depended on to say sooner or later to a cartoonist is "I saw what you drew, but what do you really think?" I do see it must be irritating. What's everybody doing?' He looked at them with some concern, and then his voice got more drawling as it did when he had amused himself. 'I mean, I can see how you're behaving, but what are you really doing?'

Harry walked out into the garden. Don looked after him and said 'What's the matter with him?'

'Us, I should think,' said Kakia. 'Especially you.' She ran out after Harry. He was looking at an empty flower bed and smoking. 'Are you all right?' she said.

'I felt stifled, that's all. Do you think he's going to go on wrecking every other weekend for ever? It doesn't ever seem to be very enjoyable any longer.'

'Is it because of me being there?'

'It's even worse when you're not.'

'He seems to detest us both. I don't know. What was all that stuff about polygamy? He's so trite all the time and doesn't even sound as if he means it. He used to have such an ear. Why is it that the triteness of people you don't agree with is so hard to put up with? You'd think it might be gratifying but it's even worse than the triteness of yourself.'

'He's frightened of everyone he meets now. Even you,' said Harry. 'I suppose everyone behaves hideously when they're frightened of other people. We should be frightened of ourselves.'

'I am.'

'What about, particularly, now?'

She hesitated. 'I think it's because of having thoughts about someone I'm fond of that he won't let me tell him about.'

'He makes me angry, but don't let me infect you. He's just in a bad time perhaps. I'm making too much of it.'

'You don't infect me. I've got a quite separate set of feelings about him. Roughly the same, but not yours. Let's go back.'

Don too made an effort and his tone at dinner was quite different, though there was a point when he started badgering again.

'What's happened about the university?'

'They pulled out because they suddenly realised we weren't married and the dean said it would be a bad example for the students.'

'Well, that's easily remedied, isn't it?'

'I didn't think so, though I hadn't entirely made up my mind against it. I thought that if they were as conventional as all that I wouldn't have much to offer them.'

Ambrose said: 'But surely every other posh don at Oxford and Cambridge has girls going, hasn't he?'

'But this is a modern university and that's often more reactionary,' said Harry. 'And the Oxford dons don't usually live with their girls, do they? They just visit. Whereas Kakia and I carry on as if we were married! That's the immoral part of it, I gather.'

'I still don't see why you don't just get married,' said Don.

'Wait. I forgot to tell you the next bit. They had a council meeting and then they sent an emissary who got very red in the face and embarrassed and said that if marriage was against my principles it would be all right for Kakia to change her name to mine by deed poll, as long as the students didn't know about it.'

Don suddenly cracked at last and gave a real laugh and stopped bickering. 'I'm sorry,' he said. 'Oh yes, I see that. But you were looking forward to it. You're quite right, of course.

What will you do? Surely it's possible to fight it out. To do the job and not be married.'

'After I'd thought about it I thought it might be even better not to do the job and be married,' said Harry conversationally, as though he were saying nothing in particular. 'I can do something else. I've got some research going that's rather interesting.'

He hadn't even said his first sentence to Kakia. Ambrose and Don were both surprisingly romantic and excited and they had a sort of celebration. When the children were brought downstairs even Don found them enjoyable. They were wearing red flannel nightdresses and reeled about blissfully like discharged Father Christmases. Don's girlfriend had gone up to bed.

'That was lucky,' said Kakia afterwards.

'I put a sedative in her whisky, like Don's horse.'

'You didn't.' It seemed very unlike him. He looked slightly ashamed but also extremely pleased with himself.

'I tanked her up good and full of booze first so she wouldn't notice and then put some sugar in to counteract the taste. I tried it first and it certainly wasn't very well disguised, but she's a rather unobservant girl, isn't she?'

XVI

They went on seeing Don almost as often as ever. He had become an actors' agent, acquiring power and a taste for more and more of it. The job seemed to use his gifts, which were generally regarded as being an impresario's, though Ambrose once said acidly that they were more like a Stalin's who happened not to be able to stand the sight of blood; so Harry did his best to stifle his feeling that Don had turned to flesh-trading. It was better than his convulsive efforts to put together imaginative television programmes. Sometimes it went well when they saw each other, sometimes haltingly. Don had enough insight to know that he had nearly ruined two friendships, but all the same he never again wanted badly enough to retrieve them by finding a way of speaking directly. It was a difficulty he had always had, but the mannerism was made much more aggressive and flashy by his growing smart alienation from himself. The more he quoted other people and recited hip pieties about relentlessly swinging topics, the more strangled and self-isolating his voice became. A doctrinal Marxist might have wrapped his dilemma up as the product of years of living off ten per cent of other people; and as far as such explanations go it would probably have been to the point. To Kakia it happened to be bitterly like the effect of official thinking and coat-turning on Andrzej. What happens to a man when he systematically practises duplicity upon himself? When he regularly says what he feels to be hollow, thinks what strikes him as stale and supports what has never nourished him?

Don began to have stupid wrangles with them both about trivial things, usually to do with their standing to the past, perhaps because he was engaged in trying to repudiate his own. Kakia would say something about, oh, sliced bread; and Don would be perfectly ready to agree with her that it tasted like Tampax and made foul toast, except that he feared that if he did he would be on the side of putting the clock back.

So instead he said: 'Sometimes you talk as if you wanted to restore the groat. Sliced bread is part of the modern welfare state.'

'Oh, come off it. It's part of profits for flour merchants and where's-the-bread-knife.'

'More's produced.'

'More but rotten, when it could be more and good. And do you know why it isn't? Because it isn't cooked by a human being with the simple authority to taste it and make it better. Just as no real person can possibly have chosen the design of the new train compartments, which is why they've got arm-rests lower than any human arm ever reached, and fixed so that they can't be moved to make room for an extra person when it's crowded.'

'And another thing,' said Harry affably to stop her. But the next time they were with Don he fell into the same trap himself.

'They've pulled down Lady Hamilton's house,' he said sadly.

'I suppose you're against the decimal system,' said Don.

'Have you swallowed Peter Thorneycroft or something?' said Harry. 'Of course I'm not. As long as decimals help people and don't just make things easy for computers.'

'You don't really want to tear up London, do you?'

'Yes. The whole thing.'

'All right if we did it to build Brasilia or Chandigarh,' said Kakia.

'What's Chandigarh?'

'Corbusier's city in the Punjab. But if we pull down London, which we will, it won't be rebuilt by serious architects for people to live in, it'll be done by hacks for speculating thugs.'

'What are you doing about it, then?' said Don, which was unjust, because they did both try; but their efforts seemed so paltry in the face of his empire-building that Kakia said 'nothing'. It was silly and banal to talk like this and each of them felt fruitless and ashamed of it. But as soon as they were with Don again the style seemed inescapable; one of them would say something inconsequential, he would make a deduction from it that traduced it, and the old course of letting it go would no longer be possible, because it seemed a concession to his own evasiveness.

'I'm not happy about you,' said Harry to Don late one night at the cottage. His voice was always very low. His patients used to have to crane to hear it. It was so quiet at the moment that it was only just audible. Kakia was playing demon patience on the kitchen table with the weekend girlfriend, who was a Tibetan.

'You behave sometimes as if you feel you're flying apart,' he said. 'Is that right?'

Don looked at him mockingly and lit a cigarette. The sound when he puffed it was always very loud, something like a swimmer snatching breaths while he is doing the crawl.

'You never let anyone ask you about yourself any longer,' said Harry, trying to make it a statement and not a complaint. 'It was never easy, but now it seems impossible.'

Don puffed again twice and looked amused. 'I'm a rather new kind of actor's agent with a lot to do and a great deal of energy to spare. You don't approve but you're quite nice about it. You always are. Anything else?'

'What are all these bloody girls here for always?'

'So you object.'

'No, of course not. But if there was only even one I could get to know. We've always got a stranger in the room with us. I hardly ever see you on my own now. Have you ever brought the same one twice?'

'Linda, for instance. Mary Lou.'

'Well, yes. At least I can't remember which Linda was. Mary Lou was the one who passed out after she'd taken hashish, is that right?'

'You disapprove because I'm promiscuous, obviously! We've always disagreed about this.'

'That's simply not true.' In his head Harry could hear Don's voice long ago talking freely about Christabel: 'I'd marry her in cold blood, I know everything about her and I know it'd probably be hell on ice, but I'd give up everything for it'; and he remembered very well his own reply: 'Yes, but for goodness' sake have a girl or two as well, you're taking it on as if she's some sort of hairshirt.'

Don remembered this too with half his consciousness, but the other half re-wrote history and resented Harry's forbearance, so they stumbled to a stop.

'I see why you used to be so good with patients,' said Don eventually. He happened to have no intention of cruelty or sarcasm in saying it; in fact he had a hope of persuading Harry to reveal his loss in giving up medicine, perhaps even in a spirit of making up for the incapacity to admit his own sense of wastage. But Harry naturally could not discern this, and took it that he was being told that he had been patronising or officious.

'I'm sorry. I didn't mean to have a bedside manner.'

'More like across a desk in out-patients.' For the mis-understanding by then was irredeemable and Don chose to compound it. 'Like one of your hysterical mums.'

'That's rather a libel. They're not usually hysterical.'

'Do you miss it?'

'Yes, of course. But there are other things.'

'With people who are less demanding.'

'One of the things I really can't stand about my own profession is the way dootors grumble about patients being demanding. I used to find that patients will put up with murder before they made a fuss. We forget how long it's often been before they come to us. Doctors are always saying to them "Come back and see me if it doesn't get any better." But they've probably only come in the first place because it already hasn't. Do you know that the deaths from peritonitis are higher at weekends because people don't like being a nuisance?'

They could both hear the cards slapping in the kitchen and the girls exclaiming. Harry called Kakia a girl in his head, and then said to himself that she was thirty-eight, and then again that it didn't make any difference. He imagined what she looked like, with her small tough hands whisking about and her comedian's sombre face and her hair probably flying up from her face even more than usual, because she would be putting her fingers through it when she was taking a breath in the game. Then he felt wretched: the blaze of the fire was beating on his calves and the dislike of his old friend on his face, and this dislike from a man he had loved, which must probably be rooted in a just contempt for some familiar failing of slow-wittedness or sloth, so took the backbone out of him that he had a very large whisky to keep up his strength and then said:

'I suppose you think I drink too much. Booze is much better than pills, you know.'

Don was quite ignorant of medicine and could never resolve with himself whether Harry's untypicality as a doctor was admirable or deplorable, since he had a hidden fellow-regard 'for the tyranny of the more augustan type of physician who approached sickness with a little majesty, but at the same time felt a duty to respect a dissenter. However, in, this case he knew where he stood. He was devoted to pills, of which he had many drawers and shelves full, and if he knew anything about the acreage of trouble within his corpse it was that highly coloured spansules did a lot more good than drink, which made his head ache, and his feet spin like a seal's flippers on a beach ball, and everything turn miserably buzzy.

So he said: 'You talk like a quack.'

It was so vilely coarse of him that he was sorry for it at once. On Harry's face he read impatience and at last vexation.

'Those girls are driving me mad,' said Harry, leaning back and shutting his eyes and wanting to moan. He meant to get drunk, if he could, and started calculating the amount of high proof alcohol in the house. He was afraid there would hardly be enough by the time he had poured out the whisky for Don's girl that she would certainly leave, as they always seemed to nowadays. He felt rather old and suspected gout in the lobe of his ear, which is an extremefully painful place to have it and not at all funny if you are concerned in it.

Harry and Kakia had known more terrible events, more destructive, more consequential and more grievous, but none more corrosive than the slipping of their two friendships with Don. Two or three times he tried to prove to them that he had pondered about it too, by analysing what had happened between them as a disagreement on principle between someone who welcomed the future and two people who preferred the past; but it was as 'casuistic a rationalisation as either of them could imagine, and the self-righteousness of the way he offered it was not very likeable.

'You hate technology,' he said to Kakia.

'Of course I don't. It's essential. I just don't want to have it erected into a principle of civilisation like the Virgin Mary.'

'Why not?'

'Because it'll be disappointing.'

'It's because you can't commit yourself to it.'

'What a thing to be religious about.'

'You won't accept that it's a different age. In France they understand it. Paris is the most modern capital I know. It's far ahead of New York. It's the only city where I feel really at home. All the people in Paris who are doing anything interesting are living in a different world. It's totally new and exciting.' Yet his voice sounded quite dead.

'And they've got de Gaulle,' she said.

'The new generation in Paris had made the great ethical discovery. *The* discovery. That there's no need any longer to do anything you don't want to do. You should only do what you like.' In this sort of way he could make her feel as if she really were obsolescent, and Harry too, for they had both spent – wasted? – a good part of their lives doing things they didn't want to do at all, such as tinkering away hopelessly at a poor marriage instead of being decisive and cutting out, leaving Poland to work in jobs that led nowhere, aborting babies, abandoning medicine. But it was hard now to imagine Don doing anything so unpurposeful. The time of falling unguardedly in love with Christabel had gone. Doing something that you didn't want to do, that might even take you diametrically away from getting on, would seem to him a failure of drive and an offence against the self, a modern sin equivalent to the moral defect of allowing yourself to get fat. Don would never have any trouble with the nagging little dilemma of putting on flesh that he disliked because of giving himself licences that he liked. He wanted to be lean, so he simply was, like the ambitious, parch-faced girls whom he now brought down. Obviously it was a question of making up your mind. Girls didn't make up their faces any longer, apart from their eyes; they made up their minds, which was obviously a more serious and resourceful thing to do altogether. Though Harry and Kakia both still thought that they might be right, neither of them *felt* as if they were any longer. That wisp of comfort had quite gone.

'You're getting old,' Don said accusingly one summer evening in 1966 when Harry had taken off his shirt to play ping-pong on the lawn. 'Your legs are still all right, but you're getting flabby. You look like an alderman. It looks *awful*. You should take exercise.'

'I always mean to get up early and go for walks at weekends, but Kakia doesn't like walking much and in the end I seem to stay in bed and talk. Or just stay in bed. I do have a Turkish bath sometimes.'

'They're no good. You should play squash.' Don had a squash coach twice a week and went skiing every winter. When he came down to spend one of his new curtailed weekends with them he had started going for twenty-mile rides on his own, often missing lunch and coming back complaining, that he couldn't get tired.

'There's a rave piece about him in the papers' said Kakia one morning when they were reading in bed with the twins at the other end. Kakia naturally read all the papers everyday and the children liked them too, for their own reasons, such as printer's ink, rustle, aggression and also reading, for Kakia and Harry had taught them to read when they were two and a half. The girl had done it the quicker, as they expected; the boy still slept hugely and seemed to enjoy muttering and private oratory more than reading. When he was four he had had a period of screaming his head off and it seemed eventually that the best thing to do when it happened was to leave him without a public to sort it out with himself. 'Somebody should come and stop me making this bloody din,' Harry had heard him saying severely to himself one day in the middle of a tantrum. 'Bloody cheek,' Kakia had said when Harry told her, and looked worried. 'Do you think he's getting bossy?'

'What does it say?' said Harry about the article.

'That all the other agents in London are either admiring or catty about him but they have to admit that he's a phenomenon and that he's probably the most powerful agent there's ever been because he has taste and believes in himself and only sleeps six hours a night. It ends up saying that what irritates them about him is that though he's no cleverer than they are he's ten times more successful. It really is meant as a compliment.'

She felt chilled to the bone and got up to try to shake it off. They had moved from Broad Court to a house in Battersea that was quite near Ambrose's. Harry was teaching physiology and doing some research, but without any clear idea of what it might amount to, and the piece about Don drove home to him that he really had no organisation to his life at all. He could die tomorrow and be exposed as the most muddled man imaginable; whereas Don's life, whatever you might think about it, expressed the clearest purpose and quite obviously knew where the tracks were. He suddenly had a picture of himself as an old trolley-bus put out to grass in a field, groping about with his electric wires like antennae for an old route that nobody was using any longer. And then he wondered if the courses that teach you to read more quickly are any good at teaching you to think more quickly. Don had told him once at Oxford that when he was making a speech he couldn't get his thoughts out fast enough and that they piled up behind his tonsils like logs behind a weir. Harry had found this one of the most astounding things he had ever heard, and he still did. In his experience you could wait for an hour or two and be lucky if a twig floated by, and the chances of it happening at the moment when you were on your feet to make an unprepared speech were so remote as to be miraculous.

And Kakia, standing at the window gently kicking a twin out of her road like the train of an evening dress, thought with resentment and admiration about the luck of a man who only needed six hours sleep a night, and how much more she might be able to get done if she were physically the same. Though probably she would still need eight hours of time to get it, she thought despondently, because she took so long to go off and kept surfacing. Don slept instantly and solidly. She thought about this fact for a while with more affection. And at the same time she was thinking of a drawing about Vietnam, and when she could go there, and China and Mao-tse-tung's mouth, which was very like Peter Thorneycroft's to draw and oddly jammy, and Don's evident boredom with the routine of her life.

She should take some time off, think, draw more, get at the core of it.

What core?

Beside the picture of Don's life, which began to be chronicled so inescapably in newspapers and magazines, that it seemed to be hanging everywhere like sky-writing, each of them felt that they frittered hopelessly. This was the effect he had on people. The fact that he spread disquiet was an irrelevance that nobody up-to-date drew attention to. Harry saw no release from two opposing opinions about all this that shouted across the chamber of his head like some unending political brawl: that to be disquieted at all only proved once again what a mess his own personality was, and alternatively that if he had been a more forgiving man he would have been able to make Don want to live differently.

It had one effect on Kakia at least. It made her summon herself and go back to see Poland. Don was mildly intrigued and came round to see them in London the night before she went. He had a message that he wanted her to give to an actor in Warsaw without fail, saying that he was to telephone at once.

'I'll do my best,' she said, suspecting that the urgency was rather unreal. 'Suppose he's away? Wouldn't a letter do? I could take that with me and then he could decide whether or not to ring up himself. Can he afford it?'

'He can transfer the charge.'

'Can you do that from Warsaw?'

'I've no idea, darling,' he said, and laughed once like a malign shout. 'He's got to get in touch, that's all. Tell him it's a chance of the most *marvellous* part *ever* and he's the *only* actor in the *world* who could do it.' He paused and thought. 'Then if you really can't get on to him, get on to –' and he gave her another name, and looked opaque when she laughed at him.

'You'll hate the place,' he said. 'It's absolutely dead now. You should have come with me.'

'How do you know that?'

'I went last spring and there was nothing. It's all in Prague now. Prague is the only place in Europe I really feel at home.'

'I thought you only liked Paris. Last time it was Paris. You never told me you went. When?'

'Poor little Poland.'

'Don't tell me there's an in-touch thing in Communist countries now. Oh dear. You talk as if it were some pathetic mistiming of taste to go to Poland.' She fetched them both a drink. 'Sometimes English intellectuals talk about the Communist countries they've been to as if they're gardens or souffles or something and you've always come too late to see the best of them. Poland can't be that different to when you went before. They're the same people, just finding it more difficult to do things.'

All the life's gone out of it. The only person with any originality is Mrozek and he lives in Italy.'

'How can you possibly know that?' She looked at him and made a face and went on packing. She was trying to get everything into an overnight bag and a portfolio so that she wouldn't have to wait in airports while the baggage was unloaded. Don sat on the bed and watched, managing mysteriously to make it seem a rather squalid undertaking. She muttered to herself mutinously in her head.

'You remind me of – I can't remember. Damn,' he said!

'Something you said.'

'I haven't said anything interesting all evening,' she said. 'It must have been someone else. Who did you have a drink with?'

'That's it. How clever of you.' He really did think it was; in fact he admired her enormously and sometimes fancied that his new manner had something Polish about it. On the other hand he had no idea at all how she functioned. He thought her inner life almost as baffling as Harry's, and it slightly irritated him to find the result impressive when the motives were nothing he would want.

There was suddenly a burst of dog-scratching next door and a bottle broke. Kakia did something about it. He had bought two elk-hounds today that he had been photographed with in a men's fashion magazine and he had locked them up in the bathroom.

'I took them to the Ritz,' he said. 'I'm rather mad about them.'

'Who'll look after them?'

'I'll take them to the office. We'll go for enormous walks in St James's Park. I'm going to start a chain of men's boutiques selling beautiful clothes and beautiful dogs. I've made up my mind.' Made up his mind.

'What else?' she said.

'I'd like to start a magazine like a pirate radio station. Outside the law. Everything a copy, a shameless, guiltless swipe, but better and quicker and cooler than the original. I'd like to be the most brilliant plagiarist in England. Like Picasso. The right to plagiarise is one of the most important principles of life. Now I imagine you're going to be stuffy.'

'I suppose it depends how good you are. If you're second-rate like me, plagiarism would only get in the way.' He was stricken. He had always thought she was first-rate. Did she really think she wasn't? Was she right? It shook him badly. He wouldn't have dreamt of pursuing it; about this question he had the same sort of decorum as another man might have about someone's confidence that he thinks he may be sterile.

She went on packing. 'When I listen to you talking I realise that I've got no will power at all,' she said.

'It's practicality,' he said. 'It's the new virtue, the only one worth having.'

'What do you mean, new? People have always been quite practical, on and off, haven't they?'

'1956 went on about it, 1966 gets on with it.'

'What on earth does that mean?' She had misunderstood him for the moment because to her 1956 meant Poland and Hungary, but to him it was England.

'It was a frightfully dreary time. People were always saying things didn't work. The Tory Party didn't work because of Suez and the West End theatre didn't work because of class and the cinema didn't work because it was all about the war and Western Europe didn't work because it was run by old men and people didn't work because they didn't pay attention to each other.'

'Doesn't it seem to have anything to do with you any longer at all?' She asked him this carefully, after a pause, hoping for an answer, hut he replied at once:

'Not a thing. It was a mood and it's gone.'

'Not a mood. You make it sound as if the whole of Europe only existed subjectively for English writers to blow their tops about.'

'Darling, the only thing that ever makes me think of the past is the sight of you carrying on. You don't belong now, do you? You behave like a displaced person.'

'I suppose that's probably what I am,' she said.

'You're a refugee in a city of PVC gear and discothèques.'

'Hell, I wear the stuff. It's steamy but the colours are nice. London isn't all bang up-to-date anyway. You sound like *Time* magazine. There are old slums and old laws and old libraries and quite a lot of old people over twenty-two like you and me.' This was an accidentally cruel cut to him and she regretted it.

'What's the matter? Why are you so jumpy?'

'I'm sorry. Sometimes you make me feel like a specimen.'

When someone made an accusation to him he never defended himself with denials. Instead he would rephrase it himself in an exaggerated form, looking keenly interested and blowing smoke, so that the original judgment contained in it at once seemed entirely subjective and arbitrary. So he said:

'I'm a brilliant spectator. That's why I'm successful, and am going to get better and better at it. When I see an attitude I hound it back and find out what it reminds me of.' He saw no one now as unique. People in his presence had no rights of self-ownership; they were items of evidence leading to *his* conclusions. He waited alertly for them, to say something that he could enlarge upon, and generalisation to him genuinely was larger and more significant than any particular person he was observing.

Kakia said: 'When you said people used to go on too much about things not working, do you think they work now?'

He shrugged and looked uninterested. He had said it only a few minutes ago, but it was already part of the past and no longer anything to do with him. He heard the dogs scratching and suddenly wrote out a cheque to Harry for £500 and said 'I always forget to pay you for the animals. It was far far too much and she was very angry.

'You can't pay him off. I'm going away, but will you see he's all right? Of course you won't. I don't suppose you'll even ring up until you want to find out if there's a message about your wretched actor. You were better at inventing fun than anyone I knew and now you hoard everything you've got for work. What's happened to you? You used to care for him. You never have any time.'

'That's what life's like, Kakia:

'No it bloody isn't. It doesn't have to be like that at all.'

'You're being unrealistic. We're all too busy, and we do different things.'

'*You're* too busy. We always did different things. It was good before. You wrecked it and squandered it. All right, I know it can't be salvaged. I'm not arguing about that. But I'm tired of not being able to say things to you and angry to be dumped and I think about you and write letters to you that I tear up again and again. When I start it because I think you're unhappy, and I remember you giving Christabel those terrible lines, and I try to tell you that it's very dear to me why I admired and loved you and that it hasn't vanished and never could. And I try to tell you the sort of man you seem now, to other people and how you elude them and give pain and shrug them off. And I write pages of it and do it badly, and come out in a sweat, and even after half a page I know I'm never going to be able to send it because it will be an intrusion that won't even wound you any longer, only bore you or waste your time or make you sneer. I've got one in my drawer. I'll show you.' She went to her desk and found the letter in a hurry to see if she could read him any of it. It began 'I can't get your face out of my mind and keep drawing it. You look so white and disconnected –' She threw it away and sat on the bed with her back to him.

'I suppose I was trying to say that when you talk I simply don't believe you any longer. I don't mean that you lie. I mean –. You keep saying you're happy but it's like a commercial. I don't believe all this energy of yours. I think it's fabricated. Do you have any idea how chilling it is? Your sort of go and optimism is far, far more deadening than the optimism in Soviet tractor pictures. Every time you say how exciting something is it sounds like nothing but next week's poor dead duck. Your enthusiasms have more hidden disparagement than I can tell you, and sometimes they sound like the voice of everyone who ever gets into the newspapers at the minute. What are we going to do about it? You'll say I'm being parochial and that it doesn't matter but I really don't think so. If something happens somewhere it happens in a lot of places. The Spanish Civil War once seemed a long way from everywhere but it wasn't for very long. It does matter that all the politicians and fashion photographers and pace-makers who say they're excited by things in England sound cruel and worn out, and that the only people who sound at all human are the ones who don't hope for very much. It's the same in art. Everything's inside out. Optimistic art seems bitterly weary and it's despair that has some spirit. You think it isn't a dilemma?'

It was very characteristic of his disparaging and effortless modern skill that he should have simply gone away at some stage in all this and left her to it; when she turned round she was on her own. The weapon to hand her was bathos, and she had used it on herself perfectly.

XVII

She went first not to Warsaw but to stay by herself in a small town near Lodz. Don was in her mood like a thorn and for a few days she found it hard to be rid of him. She would draw and listen to people and laugh at stories, and then at night rehearse cures for the three of them at home and fret. It was ludicrous: she was in Poland after eighteen years, and a piece of London blight had settled on her so that it was all she could attend to. What let her off the hook in the end was not distance, or speaking Polish, or even the things she saw that seemed good or bad about the country. It was simply the ease of living in a small town that was not at all famous yet still seemed unchafed by any neurosis that it was peripheral. Don was such a metropolitan that it was surely absurd to imagine that he had this neurosis himself but the thought kept occurring to her that he was in the grip of some nightmare of being parochial and believed in a golden centre of power that was never quite where he was.

She stayed near Lodz for three weeks and spent a week of the time in an old wooden house with a schoolteacher and his teacher wife. When they were away in the daytime she drew and talked to people a little, but mostly sat and thought. It was a long time since she and Harry had gone away together. They might have a holiday: not at the cottage. Perhaps they could come back here when his term was over.

'My darling,

I miss you sorely. I think I've finished up the descriptions. I can't think of anything else. Spent half an hour just now looking out of the window at a nice black cat on the steps wondering where he lives at night. He's always here in the daytime but about six or seven he slopes off. He looks as if he has a good character. You'd speak for him. A cat to get on with it, I think. (But not ambitious. Preserve us.) I really can't think of anything else at all except that it would be much better if you were here too. Perhaps we could do it, without the kids. Wojciec hasn't changed and his wife's nice. I think you'd like them and they speak French. We have a lot of fun. I've hit one or two blocks but they don't seem guarded. After Don, in fact, it feels more as if a ban's been lifted. You'll think I'm being Polish. Maybe I am. Perhaps if I offered the cat something to eat he might be friendly, but on the other hand he might piss off which would be a shame. I'm coming back two days earlier if I can get a seat. It's all very well but it's stupid to miss you like this when I don't have to. I've read your last two letters about twenty times. I read them on my back lying on the bed. Thank you for all of it.

K.'

At her hotel in Warsaw there were two messages. The first was from Don, to ring Jill at once, and she threw it away. The one underneath it, earlier, was from Andrzej's wife, who had heard she was here; it said that Andrzej was very ill.

When she got to the hospital he had died two hours before and been taken to the mortuary. The nurses who had looked after him that morning were off duty but the sister had his wife's address. She wondered which of them had wanted her to come. The sister said that he had had a stroke in the street a week ago and hadn't been coherent when he spoke, but then nurses always thought that. She went to see his body and stayed a long time. Apparently no one but his wife and 'children had come. He was bitterly disliked in Warsaw. He had fallen on his feet too many times. In his youth, in a part of Poland that was now Russian, he had been intensely anti-Semitic and practically a Fascist. He had a grand Russian mother, and Kakia thought for a while of how much he must have been detested at school for his historically oppressive blood. In 1936 he had become a Stalinist, when the Communist party was illegal. He had sheltered in Russia, and when the war began he became a useful Soviet officer. At the same time his family was deported to a Russian labour camp and all but his sister died. In 1943 he was parachuted in Warsaw and that year married Kakia, who was seventeen and fighting in the underground. When the pro-Soviet Lublin Government had outwitted the London government-in-exile he started vilifying the non-Communist underground as pro-Nazi, which was something that a great many other Polish Communists found hard to forgive in a country fiercely proud that it had never produced a Quisling. To proclaim this correct attitude he became a poor novelist and a powerful cultural official, which earned him the lasting malice of other writers. In good time he was for Gomulka and even urged freedom for Catholicism, which he believed in privately but had dropped in public. Even officially he was mistrusted, In spite of his posts abroad as a showpiece cosmopolitan, and his staff loathed him, for sometimes his grand blood spurted up and he bawled at them viciously. But Kakia had known him, to be different – of course: or why would she have gone to Rome when he asked? And this time he hadn't been playing, if it really was he who had thought of asking for her, and she hadn't come in time. He looked throttled and quite unreal, like an effigy on top of a tomb. She wept not because she was unhappy but because he had seemed hardly more real when he was alive. She had never seen a man before who had died naturally. She was accustomed to corpses that looked smashed, not preserved, and to people who had died in positions of life. A replica that was as perfect as this, arranged after death by others, was more unknowable and more pitiful.

She went to see his wife. One of Andrzej's children opened the door, looking shockingly like him. His wife was sitting on an upright chair in the drawing-room near the door a chair that didn't look as if it was meant for use; she seemed to be there by accident, and she was still in the same place when Kakia left. Kakia thought it was probably her impulse to have telephoned, not his, though she was never sure. If so it was good of her to have done it.

Harry drew more out of her about Andrzej than she expected to be able to answer. About Don he stayed silent, and so did she. Two or three nights running she had a dream about Andrzej and woke up distressed and guilty.

Harry knew what it was about and accepted it, though it would have been natural if he had felt excluded by it or attacked her for nostalgia. He had more amplitude of character than anyone she knew.

A few weeks later, in a hired car driving themselves from Newcastle airport to Hexham, they quarrelled about Don. Harry had started worrying about him and saying they should do something.

'Write it off, do you hear? *Write it off.*' Kakia was shouting and the skin round her nose had gone white.

'How can you write off twenty-five years?' She stopped the car on the moors and got out. She looked as if she might walk back to Newcastle. He left her alone, finding it very difficult, and after a time she came back.

'What was all that?' he said.

'You have to drop things.'

XVIII

They were going to see his aunt and her husband. Harry had wanted her to meet them for a long time. He said they were the only members of his family he had ever liked much. They were very elderly now and lived in a council house just outside Hexham. They had been married secretly just before the first world war; she had been a suffragette, and in those days he was a miner. She came of a much richer family, which had shamed her because she was a Socialist, but she discovered that she had working blood in some cousins and went north secretly to find them, using a different name and studying them humbly. Her name was Deirdre, and her husband still thought it a joke, like her cooking, which he pretended needed a background of kitchenmaids.

She still had a pure upper-class Edwardian accent, saying 'gel' and 'yumour' and 'otel' and 'orf'. Once while Harry and Kakia were there she said 'divvy' for divide. Her husband had a throaty Northumbrian accent that Kakia sometimes found quite difficult to understand. His name was Stephen Ridley, and he had been a famous Trades Unionist. In the Great War she had grown famous and beloved in the north as a battler to found the first women's union, winning meagre concessions for munition workers who were often doing an eighty-hour week for $1^1/_2$ d an hour. The two of them had written many books together, and when they talked about political opinions they always said 'we'. It was the sort of partnership that both Harry and Kakia were usually apt to suspect, but there was no question of priggishness about it or anything secondhand. The little house where they lived was very simple and the atmosphere was gay and authentic.

Stephen was a spruce, short man with a beautiful pink complexion and a chin like a girl's heel. He wore a yellow waistcoat with a gold watch-chain across it and when they were having lunch he took off his jacket, asking Kakia first if he might. He listened to people without blinking and with his mouth a little open, praying that, they would make him laugh and chuckling helplessly whenever they said anything at all funny, with his eyes held wide open painfully all the time he was laughing in the hope that the talkers would go on and say something more. His wife was taller than he was and she seemed more remote and vague, but this was an illusion. She wore a navy blue belted suit with a long skirt and a frilly shirt that was perfectly laundered. The belt was black patent and it looked a little as if it could have held a pistol, for there was something dashing about the way she stood and the suit was like the sort of uniform in which an Edwardian woman might have fought a cause. But she was not at all formidable; on the contrary, she seemed shy, and enormously pleased they had come. They sat in the kitchen while she finished serving the lunch. It was all cooked and ready.

'That's a girdle,' said Stephen, pointing to an old black iron pan. 'Dreary calls it a griddle because she's from the south.' He called her Dreary sometimes instead of Deirdre and it seemed to make her a little cross.

'No I don't. It's a girdle.' she said.

Stephen sometimes did the cooking himself. He would make a girdle cake called a singing hinny, a big flat cake with currants in it, and ask people in to eat it on Saturday night. He loved to match-make, and listen to small-talk, and patch up fights, and take children to picnics on the Roman Wall. Last night he had baked for the twins two little dough-men with sultana faces; they were wrapped up in greaseproof paper ready to travel, in a

Coronation Cadbury's biscuit-tin that dated from before the war.

Deirdre had cooked a sirloin and Yorkshire pudding, and then there was a gooseberry fool.

'She sieved it and I whipped the cream,' said Stephen. 'Then I finished the sieving because she's got weak wrists. She's a toff, you see.' In fact both of them had arthritis that gave them much pain, but they took it in turn to do things.

In the front room there was an upright piano with a brass candelabra on it, and a television set with a small red lamp and a silver cigarette box. Inscribed to both of them. They asked Harry about the abortion case and Deirdre turned out to know the law minutely because she was on a committee to try to reform it. She had a scrupulous and detailed mind, with something stoic yet truly entertaining about her that made Kakia see her temperament in Harry. Mostly she asked questions, like him. The atmosphere was quite distinct: it was sharp-eared and not at all indulgent, yet at the time warm and convivial. Stephen kept spluttering with laughter, but there was never any bantering in it and the attention of both of them was too finely tuned to allow them to assume anyone not to mean what was said.

'Shouldn't you go back to medicine?' she said to Harry.

'The General Medical Council would surely reinstate you.'

I'm not anxious to rest on their favours.'

'Yes. And you'll have done something else by now.'

She had the same basis to the composition of her features as Harry had, especially in her eyebrows and the bones over her eyes. Kakia tried to reconstruct a picture of his father from the sight of the two of them together. Her voice was very low, like Harry's, with a slight upward inflection that made it naturally inquiring.

Stephen and Deirdre asked her about Poland and it was often comically difficult to remember which of them was speaking.

'It was a brilliant achievement,' said Dierdre. 'Gomulka understood exactly what to do, didn't he?'

'It had to be very precise,' said Stephen.

'We were afraid that he was going to let the failure of the Hungarian Revolution push the people too far. Krushchev couldn't have allowed it.'

'To keep Krushchev circling in the air over Warsaw for an hour while he made up his government!' said Stephen in awe, with his eyes as wide as for a joke. 'Rokossovsky had to go, he knew that. Everything finished and assessed before permission to land. What a stroke. When we read about it, it made us think of the mess Kerensky made in 1917:

'When Kerensky was going through those rituals with Kornilov and conducting foolish little discussions about switching seats in the government. It was the Bolsheviks' great chance to step in, of course, wasn't it?' Deirdre started to laugh in her high-backed chair. 'Trotsky said Kerensky was like someone discussing the positions in a sleeping berth.'

'You never told me that,' said Stephen, after gasping with laughter in his seat and shaking for a time and watching her like a hawk in the hope of more.

'Tell Kakia about father,' said Harry.

Deirdre brought down a black deed box. She had a photograph in it of her brother when he was about five, taken at some seaside place; Eastbourne or Frinton or Swanage probably, for those were the branch addresses listed under the photographer's name. It was quite a formal portrait; he was leaning on a cricket bat in the sand and smiling, because it was a photograph to be sent to his own father, who was in South Africa fighting in the Boer War. When, the old gentleman had died many years later – long after his own son, who was mortally ill by the time Harry was nine – Deirdre had had to clear up his papers and found he had kept the picture in his crocodile wallet. She also had a photograph of her brother's wedding in 1921, with old-fashioned policemen holding back a crowd outside a church, and tiny page-boys in satin breeches and ruffled shirts who were being sheltered from the rain by a rank of nurses in long uniforms with big black umbrellas.

'We weren't there,' said Stephen. 'It was a grand church, you can see that, can't you? It was at St George's church in Hanover Square.'

Charles wanted us to come but our mother didn't permit it. It wasn't that she objected to Stephen, you understand. It was the fact that I had been in prison when I was a suffragette.'

'You'd wonder how they could do it,' said Stephen. 'She was fed by tube up her nose, thirty-two times. They were bound in a sheet in a feeding chair and one doctor held them while another operated the tube. You can't think of it. When we met each other her voice was quite different. It was like a man who'd been gassed in the war because her throat was so swollen. And she has claustrophobia, you know. She went to prison with that. She never told them at headquarters.'

'Charles was a little boy at school then,' said Deirdre. We used to write to each other until my mother suspected it and stopped it. Once I took him out to tea, though I wasn't supposed to. I took him down to the East End and he saw what it was like. The women tried to feed him up because he was as thin as they were. I suppose he must have been ill already. When he was a grown man he used to come up to see us both quite often. He would tell his wife it was business, and give her the names of the firms the contracts were supposed to be with, and they were the names of all the left wing politicians she wouldn't have had in the house! She really wasn't very alert, was she Harry?'

'Once he brought Harry up, to see us, when he was a little boy of four or five,' said Stephen. 'We made him a kite. We laughed all the time.'

'He and Stephen got on so well,' said Deirdre. 'When Charles died we asked his wife to let us look after Harry because he had once said he didn't think she was very fond of hun, but she never replied to our letters. Do you know, we were so angry with her after twenty-five years of it that when the Second World War broke out we arranged to have her house requisitioned for billets. She blushed. 'We did a little string-pulling.' 'The place was far too big for her,' said Stephen.

'But all the same she made quite a bother and in the end we decided I should go to the house and see to it myself. I had the authority you see. And I said our name quite quietly, and kept my temper, and she bolted upstairs like a filly and shot messages out at me on the lawn by a catapult. She had very little sense of humour, you see, hadn't she, Harry? I'm afraid I went up there in the end and shook her by the shoulders and just said "a-po-lo-gise" over and over again. I've never done such a thing in my life. I suppose that technically it constituted an assault, didn't it? Well, never mind now. I got her to sign the requisition form, and while I was about it I got a note out of her apologising to Stephen.'

She had such a gentle voice that it seemed funny, but plainly the feelings had been very fierce at the time. She made tea for them and they had to have some of Stephen's raisin cake.

'Nearer the coal-fields a singing hinny's called a sma' coal fizzer,' he said, cutting it for them lovingly. 'You make them on fires that are kept in with small coal. Small coal's cheaper and lasts longer. The cakes fizz when they go on the girdle. It's a better description than singing really.'

'Will you bring your children up to see us one day?' said Deirdre. 'If you think they would like it?'

Stephen said that they wanted to leave their books to the twins in their wills. 'We thought of giving them to the library and then we decided against it. They wouldn't mean very much if they were split up and the public libraries are well stocked up now. Oh! no! *jam, jam,*' he said, seeing Harry have a scone without jam.

'We're making a catalogue so they know where to find things. Our notebooks are there as well, you see. We should have to see if we couldn't find some of Harry's old toys if the children were to come up here to see us. I believe we might have kept the kite, you know. When they learnt to read I expect it was with the system of very large letters printed in red, wasn't it? I think I read some papers about using it on children with brain-damage. How long each day did you do it for?'

She wanted to know everything about it. Later she gave Harry one more snapshot of his father that he had never seen, showing him waving outside a railway station and smiling broadly with a newspaper in his hand.

'I'm afraid I didn't focus it very well,' she said. 'We were coming to meet him in Newcastle in a motor car and we were a little late and I suddenly saw him. He had some good news for us.' She smoothed the little yellow snapshot with her fingers. 'Perhaps you could get it enlarged. It's very like him, isn't it?' She had taken it out of her bag, where it was kept in a little celluloid holder. Plainly she looked at it often but she gave it to Harry in a spirit that was near aplomb and Kakia saw that he found it difficult not to weep.

Before they left, Stephen took Harry for a walk round Hexham and made him come into a pub for a drink. On the way back, he said: 'This year our age is a hundred and fifty-nine. Our joint age, I mean.'